GIRL SHADOWED

An addictive and gripping crime mystery thriller

Detective Kaitlyn Carr
Book 8

KATE GABLE

Copyright

Proofreader:

Renee Waring, Guardian Proofreading Services, https://www.facebook.com/GuardianProofreadingServices

Cover Design: Kate Gable

Visit my website at www.kategable.com

Be the first to know about my upcoming sales, new releases and exclusive giveaways!

Want a Free book? Sign up for my Newsletter!

Sign up for my newsletter:

https://www.subscribepage.com/kategableviplist

Join my Facebook Group: https://www.facebook.com/groups/833851020557518

Bonus Points: Follow me on BookBub and Goodreads!

https://www.goodreads.com/author/show/21534224.Kate_Gable

About Kate Gable

Kate Gable loves a good mystery that is full of suspense. She grew up devouring psychological thrillers and crime novels as well as movies, tv shows and true crime.

Her favorite stories are the ones that are centered on families with lots of secrets and lies as well as many twists and turns. Her novels have elements of psychological suspense, thriller, mystery and romance.

Kate Gable lives near Palm Springs, CA with her husband, son, a dog and a cat. She has spent more than twenty years in Southern California and finds inspiration from its cities, canyons, deserts, and small mountain towns.

She graduated from University of Southern California with a Bachelor's degree in Mathematics. After pursuing graduate studies in mathematics, she switched gears and got her MA in Creative Writing and English from Western New Mexico University and her PhD in Education from Old Dominion University.

Writing has always been her passion and obsession. Kate is also a USA Today Bestselling author of romantic suspense under another pen name.

Write her here:

Kate@kategable.com

Check out her books here:

www.kategable.com

Sign up for my newsletter:
https://www.subscribepage.com/kategableviplist

Join my Facebook Group:
https://www.facebook.com/groups/833851020557518

Bonus Points: Follow me on BookBub and Goodreads!

https://www.bookbub.com/authors/kate-gable

https://www.goodreads.com/author/show/21534224.Kate_Gable

amazon.com/Kate-Gable/e/B095XFCLL7
facebook.com/KateGableAuthor
bookbub.com/authors/kate-gable
instagram.com/kategablebooks
tiktok.com/@kategablebooks

Also by Kate Gable

Detective Kaitlyn Carr Psychological Mystery series

Girl Missing (Book 1)

Girl Lost (Book 2)

Girl Found (Book 3)

Girl Taken (Book 4)

Girl Forgotten (Book 5)

Girl Deceived (Book 6)

Girl Hunted (Book 7)

Girl Shadowed (Book 8)

Girl Hidden (FREE Novella)

FBI Agent Alexis Forrest Series

Forest of Silence

Forest of Shadows

Forest of Secrets

Forest of Lies

Forest of Obsession

Forest of Regrets

Detective Charlotte Pierce Psychological Mystery series

Last Breath

Nameless Girl

Missing Lives

Girl in the Lake

Lake of Lies (FREE Novella)

About Girl Shadowed

A beautiful young woman's mutilated body is found in the sand near the breaking waves of the Pacific Ocean. When Detective Kaitlyn Carr is called to the scene, she discovers that it belongs to Emilia Cruz, an actress on a popular Netflix show, who had just attended the Screen Actors Guild Awards and is still wearing her gown from the night before.

As Kaitlyn begins her relentless pursuit of the truth, she uncovers a shocking secret: Emilia had recently joined a wellness cult led by an enigmatic figure who promises enlightenment through unconventional methods. The cult's obsession with green juices and extreme food restrictions raises suspicions, but Kaitlyn's investigation takes an unexpected turn when Emilia's old high school boyfriend, hailing all the way from Iowa, emerges as a potential suspect.

Caught between the chilling possibilities of a fanatical cult and the haunting presence of an obsessed ex-lover, Kaitlyn must navigate a treacherous path to expose the true culprit. With each step closer to the truth, she unravels a dark mystery that threatens to shatter the glitz and glamour of Hollywood.

Meanwhile, as Kaitlyn delves deeper into the investigation, she finds herself standing at the precipice. With her wedding to Luke Galvinson, an FBI agent, fast approaching, Kaitlyn must balance the demands of her personal life and her pursuit of Emilia's killer.

In this page-turning psychological mystery, follow Detective Kaitlyn Carr as she tackles her most perilous case yet, unraveling a twisted tale of deception, obsession, and the high stakes of love and justice in the City of Angels.

Chapter 1

Early morning sunlight peeked over the ocean's horizon, streaks of orange and yellow painting the blue sky. Not a single soul was on the beach besides Aidan Palmer, a tan-skinned, dark-haired lifeguard who often worked the early shift. Mornings were cooler and far more peaceful than facing the afternoon heat and crowd surges.

His brown sandals knocked against the wooden stairs of the lifeguard station as he approached the front door, fishing a key out of the pocket of his red shorts. A dull throb echoed throughout his head as he shuffled inside, squinting his eyes against the sunlight. The extra tequila shot he'd had at his friend's birthday bash last night was hitting him hard and his stomach churned uneasily.

If he could get through his shift he could recover at his apartment and make better drinking choices next time. He downed half of the bottle of water that he'd brought with him with the hope that some hydration would heal him after a long night. If only things were that simple, but life didn't work that way.

Trouble brewed, in some form, every single day.

Aidan got set up for his shift, looking over all of his equipment, smearing sunscreen over his face and bare chest, and popping a pain reliever for his aching head. He started to open a protein bar to put something besides alcohol in his stomach, but something caught his green eyes out in the distance. He stepped closer to the large window at the front of the white and light blue shack-like structure focusing on some sort of shiny mass at the waterline.

It could've been a piece of driftwood, trash, or something left behind from yesterday, but what really caught his eye were the birds. Seagulls gathered, investigating it closely, some even pecking at it.

Something was up that he couldn't just ignore.

Aidan headed down the stairs to the sand, ditching his sandals in the station. His bare feet sank into the cool sand, a few shells poking at his heels as he walked toward the shoreline. The closer he got, the more wary he felt as he tried to make out what he was looking at.

The shiny color belonged to a silver sequined evening gown which was bundled up. His throat tightened as he edged closer, trying to see better through the swarm of seagulls that kept flying down to take a look as well. When he saw damp, blonde hair sprawled out across the sand, his hand clamped down on his mouth, trying to keep what he drank last night from coming back up.

"Shoo! Go!" Aidan shouted at the seagulls, waving his hands to get them to scatter.

Some of them picked at the woman's flesh, and enough of them prying at her skin had resulted in some glimpses of bone on her cheek and forearm. A few of the birds were stubborn, not budging until he nearly swatted them directly.

Once they'd cleared, he had a full view of the woman's back and side since she was curled up with her lifeless eyes facing the water. The morning sunlight reflected in their blue color, matching the water that quietly rolled onto the shore toward her. Her skin glistened with sand and water droplets, and from what he could see, she had once been beautiful.

Before death, and the birds, had claimed her.

Aidan spun around, looking up and down the beach to see if anyone was around.

Was she dumped here?

Did she wash up on shore?

If she had been, there were no trails in the sand because the water had washed them away. All that he could see was her. Or what was left of her.

"This can't be happening. Not right now," Aidan murmured as he ran his hand through his hair, his head throbbing. He swallowed hard and dug his phone out of his pocket, trying to keep his hand steady as his finger tapped the nine and the one buttons.

"9-1-1, what's your emergency?" a woman's voice sounded over the phone speaker.

"Hi, I'm at Dockweiler Beach. I just showed up for my lifeguard shift, and there's a body here," Aidan replied. It was such a gruesome sight, but he couldn't take his eyes off the dead woman, entranced by the horror.

"Can you describe the body to me? And what's your name, sir?" the operator asked.

Aidan felt bile rise up his throat.

"Um... Aidan Palmer. It's a woman. Uh... blonde hair. Young, like in her twenties. In a fancy dress," he said. "I don't think there's any blood. I don't know. The water could've washed it away."

"Have you checked to make sure that she's breathing? Or unconscious?" the operator asked.

"You want me to... check?" Aidan asked, his heart hammering in his chest. "I'm pretty sure she's dead."

"Yes, sir. Just see if she's breathing."

Aidan felt a cold sweat threaten to break out on his forehead. He glanced around like he wanted to run, but he inched closer to the woman instead.

"I don't think she's breathing. Birds have been picking at her for a while," Aidan replied as he leaned close, watching the woman's body. If she were alive, he would've seen her body rise and fall with faint breaths.

She was completely still.

"Does she have anything on her? Purse? Phone? Anything that may identify her," the operator asked.

Aidan carefully walked around the body, looking at the sand and at the water to see if anything stuck out to him. But when he got right in front of her, able to see her stomach in her curled up position, he saw something that would haunt his sleep for the nights to come.

"Her… her stomach. It's slashed open. I can see her insides," Aidan breathed out, hardly able to make his voice come out clear enough to be understood.

"Alright, officers will be on the scene shortly. Stay where you are," the operator instructed him.

Aidan nodded and took a few steps back from the woman.

"Okay, I will. How many minutes do you think?" he asked, his face starting to pale. His hangover not helping the situation.

"Just a few," the operator replied. "I'll stay on the line with you until they arrive."

Aidan turned away from the body, watching the road intently. The sooner the cops arrived, the sooner he could leave the scene of this nightmare. But nothing could match the nightmare that this woman had faced.

2

Kaitlyn

A steady stream of hot water pounds against the back of my head as I stand quietly in the shower listening to the roar of the controlled downpour. I have to leave for work in an hour, but my body doesn't want to budge from the spot. Work has been incredibly demanding lately.

I guess that's what I signed up for when I became a detective for the LAPD. I find satisfaction in what I do but it's a long road from the start to the end. There's a lot of frustration, not a lot of sleep, and typically a bunch of blood. So, some days I don't want to go to work. I just want a day of peace.

Suddenly, the curtain opens making me pull my head out of the water to turn and see my fiancé, Luke, step into the shower. His bare sculpted chest and firm biceps are a testament to his work as an FBI agent.

"Oh, hello. It's nice to see you again. It's been like a week, right?" Luke asks with a smirk as he wraps his arms around my waist, pulling my body against his.

I crack a smile and shake my head.

"Feels like it. I think I came home at midnight last night," I tell him. Both of our schedules have been so packed since we got back from the Pacific Northwest that it's a miracle we get to spend more than five waking hours together in a day. And we live together.

Luke steps under the water, his short, dark hair soon getting soaked.

"I miss you," he says as he caresses the small of my back with one hand and brushes my wet hair out of my face with his other.

I tilt my head to press my cheek into his palm, a warm sensation glowing in my chest. We've been together for years, on the cusp of getting married.

"I miss you a lot. I miss having dinner together. Or being able to watch a movie with you without falling asleep in the middle of it," I sigh.

Luke chuckles.

"In your defense, the last one we watched was pretty boring," he says.

There are many reasons why I love Luke. He's the easygoing, optimistic guy, which is probably the product of being born into a big, happy family. I lack those qualities and that background, but I'm grateful for the person he is and the support he has had even if I would probably find it a little suffocating.

"You're not wrong," I reply with a small laugh, our eyes meeting. I feel him pull me closer, his lips soon finding mine as the heat from the water surrounds us.

Luke cups my face, our kiss deepening as his teeth graze my bottom lip. He turns us and backs me up against the shower wall, mouthing at my neck.

"I really miss you," he murmurs against my skin.

I close my eyes and inhale the steam, running my fingers through his hair and losing myself in his touch. Finally, the world fades away as a hot, dizzy haze fills my head.

Luke lowers his head, putting his mouth on the nape of my neck. His free hand caresses me. It feels like he's touching me all over, not missing an inch of bare skin.

Making love with him is all-encompassing, gentle, and yet intense.

Luke grabs the underside of my leg and lifts it up. His forehead rests against mine, our shaky breaths mingling and our bodies feeling like one.

It doesn't even matter that we are not under the spray of water. My skin feels hot to the touch as he presses me against the wall, our lips meeting again. Faint moans break from me. My nails dig into his biceps as I hang onto him tightly.

"So good. You're so beautiful," he murmurs, speaking sweet words that only push me closer to the edge.

I wrap my arms around his neck, anchoring him to me. My lips find his in a slow, tingly kiss as the heat in our bodies starts to simmer down.

"That's a nice way to start the day," I say with a crooked smile.

Luke chuckles and nods in agreement.

"Oh, yeah. Noted," he replies, shooting me a cheeky grin before setting my leg down carefully. He soaps up a washcloth and starts running it over my body.

Once we dry off and get dressed for the day, we meet up in the kitchen, making coffee, scrambled eggs, and toast for breakfast. With thirty minutes left, we sit at the round dining table and open our phone calendars up. It's the only way we can get coordinated.

"So, wedding planning. We still have a lot to do. Well, more like *you* have a lot to do," Luke says. "I've already decided on my suit and booked that venue we liked."

I don't miss the slightly annoyed tone in his voice. He's not the type to argue, but his frustration is admittedly my fault. I've been dragging my feet a little with all of this wedding planning. I've been so busy lately with work, and the thought of doing things like picking out my wedding dress and finding a stylist all by myself is a bit daunting.

"What's next on the list?" I ask him.

"Cake testing," Luke replies. "Last week, we decided to go today at three in the afternoon. Can you still make it?"

"That should work," I tell him, figuring that's usually a slow point in my day.

"Alright, great," Luke says. He then turns off his phone and looks up at me, which tells me that he's about to get serious. "Remember, I have to go to Sacramento for training. I'll be gone that whole week, and we're getting down to the wire here for the wedding, so I need you to get some of your things done."

I force myself to nod and give him an assuring smile, not wanting him to stress out with training coming up.

"Sure," I reply. "I'll go to the dress store after work or get someone to cover for me for a few hours."

Luke nods.

"Sounds good. I'm sure whatever you pick will be beautiful. I wish I could be there with you."

"That would be bad luck. Or at least that's what they say," I tell him with a small smirk. I really don't know all of the traditions and rules. My mom won't be around to remind me of them, and that's honestly fine. My relationship with her is… tense. A lot has happened in my family, and being around each other is a constant reminder of that.

Even if I don't want to do everything alone, it's better this way. I don't want to feel her hard gaze on me as I try to find the perfect dress to walk down the aisle in, and I don't want any drama tainting what is supposed to be my perfect day. I can't stomach that.

"Still. I don't want to leave you," he sighs as

he sinks back into his chair. “I don’t want to go. It’s just… so much.”

I frown, hearing the exhaustion in his voice. I know that his career isn’t his favorite thing. He has even talked about quitting and pursuing something else like private investigation, but he doesn’t really have a plan as of now.

I don’t blame him. Law enforcement isn’t for the faint of heart. You have to love it to stick around, and I suppose I have some sort of masochistic relationship with it. It stresses me out and drives me up the wall, but I live and breathe for my work. I can’t see myself doing anything else.

“I know,” I tell him, reaching out to take his hand and give it a comforting squeeze.

Luke smiles a little and strokes my knuckles with his thumb.

This tender moment is broken when my phone rings. I already know it’s work.

“Detective Carr,” I say with a sigh.

“I need you at Dockweiler Beach immediately. We have a body,” Captain Medvil says.

What a lovely thing to hear first thing in the morning.

“I’ll be right there,” I reply before hanging

up. I down the rest of my coffee before getting to my feet. "Body on the beach. Duty calls."

Luke gets up and kisses me on the cheek.

"See you at Angel Maid Bakery. 3 pm," he tells me. "Don't forget."

I nod and squeeze his arm before grabbing my things and heading out to my car. I hit the road a minute later, driving toward LAX. As the ocean comes into view, so do the flashes of police car lights in the near distance. I pull over to the side of the road and park with a plane roaring overhead as it nears the runway.

Investigators already litter the sand, police tape sectioning off the portion of the beach where the body is located. I draw in a deep breath as a low ringing sound fills my ears. I know what comes next, and it won't look pretty.

3

Kaitlyn

It doesn't take long for inquisitive people and paparazzi to catch wind of a body found at Dockweiler Beach. I can hear their voices and the clicks of cameras as I stand in front of her, my eyes sweeping the scene. From what I can see, none of her belongings are anywhere in sight, but a few of the investigators are poking around in the sand and looking down the shoreline in case they have scattered in the wind.

My gaze centers back on the woman in front of me, her skin gleaming and pale. Her innards are spilling out onto the sand, and her hands are laying around her stomach like she had been trying to keep them from coming out. The water has already washed away all of the blood, but that doesn't make the scene any less gruesome.

Someone sliced her open either here or somewhere else, letting the birds have at her. My stomach twists as I crouch down to get a better look. Her gown has a form-fitting silhouette with a plunging neckline. It has a dramatic slit up the leg and the silver silk material gives it a subtle shimmer that catches the midmorning light. Around her midsection, her dress is drenched in blood.

The beach is a beautiful, peaceful place, but it's a nightmare for a murder investigation. And I can safely say that this is a murder. You could never do this to yourself.

"Now, who are you?" I murmur as I walk around to the front of her. Pictures have already been taken, but I'm still not going to move her just yet. She won't be moved until the medical examiner has a chance to take a look.

I peer at her face, my eyebrows lifting in shock. I know her! Well, not personally, but she's an actress on a sci-fi show on Netflix called *Quantum Frontier*. I literally just binged the most recent season.

Now, the lead actress, Emilia Cruz, is dead in front of me.

She's only in her twenties, projected to be one of Hollywood's newest up-and-coming stars.

"Pretty gnarly, huh?" one of the patrol cops says.

"I guess you could say that," I reply as I observe her face. There isn't any bruising, so she likely wasn't struck or hit in the head. However, from her curled up position, I can see a few dark marks on her neck. Possible strangulation.

But why slice her open? And when was that done?

Only the medical examiner can tell me that.

I straighten up and walk a few feet away from Emilia, watching some of the other investigators search the perimeter. I don't think they'll find anything, but we have to comb the scene top to bottom before moving on. Crime scenes can be tampered with quite easily, and it will be hard enough to preserve any evidence as it is.

"Woah! Woah!" another patrol cop shouts.

I whip around to see one of the paparazzi, some scrawny guy in a Hawaiian shirt and a baseball cap, sprinting over to the wet sand, his shoes splashing in the foamy waves, and snapping pictures.

"Hey! Get out of here! This is an active

crime scene!" I shout at him, watching a few patrol cops chase him off. I shake my head as my jaw tenses, glaring at the deputies. "Your job is to guard the perimeter. Eyes up!"

He shrinks away from me, hanging his head and nodding.

I bite back any other choice words, remaining as professional as possible. I hate paparazzi, though. They are literally the human equivalent of buzzards, picking away at whatever they can find to sate themselves. I'd gladly make civilians taking pictures at a crime scene illegal.

"We need more privacy. Get more tents or something," I tell the deputies, gesturing to Emilia, who is nearly out in the open for anyone to see.

I walk over to one of the investigators searching the sand, drawing in the smell of sea salt through my nose.

"Find anything?" I ask. Even if there's a piece of jewelry or a stray footprint, that can possibly help. Though footprints are almost impossible to find in the sand. Sometimes, the things that don't seem like great clues turn out to be one of the most valuable pieces of evidence.

He shakes his head and rests his hands on his stout hips.

"Nothing. Not a drop of blood or anything. There are some indentations in the sand over there that may be footprints, but they're so warped that they're basically useless," he mutters as he gestures to a spot farther away from the water.

"Well, I know she didn't come out here alone. Maybe someone saw him from the road or at least saw a car parked around here."

"Think he dumped her? Or killed her here?" The investigator asks me as we peer over at Emilia as the patrol cops put up another tent to shield her from the rest of the paparazzi still lingering around in the background.

I shake my head, wishing I had an answer. Solving a complex case is akin to piecing together a puzzle, but in this case, the puzzle has been deliberately scrambled.

"I'm going to talk to the medical examiner once she's transported. She can give me a timeline that I can work with," I tell him. "Then, I need to retrace her steps and figure out how she got to this beach in the first place."

"Just another day," he murmurs.

I look out at the water, realizing that's probably the last thing Emilia saw before she died. I doubt any part of her dying was peaceful, but I hope she had a second of peace before passing. After seeing the state of her body, that's all I can hope for.

Once the crime scene has been fully searched and she's taken away to be looked at by the medical examiner, I head back to my car to follow her there. The flash of a camera catches the corner of my eye, and I resist the urge to flip off whoever took that picture. I don't understand how people can be so insensitive.

A young woman has been killed, and all they care about is the payoff of getting a good picture.

4

Kaitlyn

After being in this job for so long, I thought I'd get used to how cold the medical examiner's room is, but the chill still jars me as I stand next to the metal table that Emilia is laying on. Bright fluorescent lights shine down on her body, her beautiful dress now gone and stored in some evidence bag. I hate seeing her like this instead of the determined, sassy space ranger in *Quantum Frontier*.

I wonder if she put up a fight against her attacker.

Or did she even have a chance to?

Dr. Berinsky, who I know simply as Laura, is three years older than I am with deep-set eyes and thin-framed glasses perched on her sharp nose. Over the years, we've become close, enjoying the occasional dinner when our busy schedules allow.

"Find anything good?"

Laura holds a clipboard in one hand that lists all of the notes that she's written down.

"There is one long, deep laceration across the entirety of her abdomen," she says as she gestures to where Emilia's stomach is split open with her black pen. "From what I can tell, most of the organs are intact, except her liver. It appears to have been removed. Look here," she points, and I force myself to look. "See this clean cut? This was done with a very sharp blade."

"Just the liver? Not the kidneys or anything?"

"No, nothing else."

Laura shakes her head.

"Nope. The only other thing I found was an indication that she was strangled, as you can see by these bruises around her neck. And there's no water in her lungs. She didn't drown."

"Alright, so what came first? Was she strangled and then cut open? Or vice-versa?" I ask, wanting to know what the fatal wound is so that I can get my timeline straight.

"Probably strangled before," Laura replies as she taps her pen against her chin.

Either fate is terrible, but it would be better if she were already dead before she was cut into.

"Then, why cut her open? He didn't take her other valuable organs or put anything inside of her," I say, speaking my thoughts aloud.

"Maybe they took something else."

"Like what? What else would be inside of her?" Laura questions me with a confused look, the wrinkles on her forehead broadening.

"A baby," I reply, making her eyes widen.

I can't rule a single thing out yet, no matter how sick and twisted. There have been cases where babies were cut out to make some sort of statement.

I wonder if she had a boyfriend and if someone else knew that she was pregnant. There have been stories in the news about women trying to steal babies right from the womb but, in those cases, the child could survive on the outside and the pregnancy would have to be far along.

"Well, we will do a full autopsy. If we find anything else of interest, I'll reach out to you and let you know," Laura promises me before looking over at Emilia with a frown. "So sad.

She was getting so popular that I couldn't open Instagram without seeing a post about her."

No one expects these types of things to happen, especially to celebrities. They seem invincible in a way with their fame and money. They're well-protected typically, but I don't remember seeing pictures of her with bodyguards. Maybe she thought she wasn't big enough to need them. Or maybe she liked her privacy.

Now, she's going to be on every front page and every news channel for the next few weeks. Everyone will know what happened to her.

"I know. I watched the show she was in. Bad things just happen so fast."

"Well, that's why there are people like us," Laura points out.

If only we were able to prevent these things from happening in the first place. Dealing with the aftermath doesn't fill the hole in my chest that gets deeper with each case. Even if we find the bad guy, someone is still dead.

If only I had Luke's optimism, maybe I could find some silver linings. He always tells me that I'm doing the families a service by getting justice for their lost loved ones. That I'm avenging the dead and keeping the bad guys from hurting anyone else.

Maybe that's true, but I wish I could do more than attend to the mess. Then again, maybe messes are my thing. My life has been plagued by them ever since I was little, and I've become an expert at sorting through them. I don't know if I believe in a determined path or a calling, but if it does exist, this would be mine.

"We'll get whoever did this to her," I say.

But it doesn't always work out like that. Some cases are never solved, and the ones I haven't been able to crack linger in the back of my mind and will continue to do so for the rest of my life. They are my failures.

I refuse to let that happen here.

5

Kaitlyn

After leaving the medical examiner's office, I head to a local bookstore. Despite the uneasy feeling in my stomach, I know that I'll need a jolt of caffeine to push me through the rest of the day. I prefer to go out in the field, but in my time as a detective, I've learned that I can figure out a lot about the case by being nowhere near the scene of the crime. I need to look at everything from an outsider's perspective.

"Cappuccino, please," I tell the barista at the tiny café toward the front of the store.

"Coming right up," the young brunette quips.

I hand her five dollars and tell her to keep the change before turning to browse a nearby magazine rack while she makes my coffee. I can't remember the last time that I picked up a magazine, but I need every piece of gossip that I can find about Emilia Cruz. She's been front page news lately with the success of her show, so it doesn't take me long to find three different gossip magazines with her smiling face plastered on the front.

E*milia Cruz's Stunning Beach Bod!*

A *Day on the Set of America's Favorite Sci-Fi Show: Emilia Cruz Tells All!*

I roll my eyes at the shallow headlines.

The only thing that I know about her is that she's an actress on a show that I like. Outside of that, I don't know if she has a boyfriend or if she has a brand deal with some sort of skincare company or if she is an avid Pilates lover. That's what I need to figure out.

All of the little details. That's where the clues are hiding.

"Cappuccino!" the barista calls out.

I walk back over to the café and pick up my cappuccino, feeling the heat through the paper cup. I nod my thanks and take a sip reveling in the brief satisfaction of its warm, bold taste. As much as I like the smell of fresh book pages and coffee, I drag myself out of the store, driving back to the office for a long bout of research.

The white plastic bag full of magazines hangs on my arm as I walk into the station, nodding to a few officers who I pass by on the way to my desk. I'm sure they've all heard about my case at this point. Rumors will spread, and unfortunately, that usually complicates the investigation. You can get a dozen false leads for every useful piece of information that comes to you from people who see the case on the news.

The problem is that innocent people are fearful of getting in trouble. If they have a piece of information that may help, a lot of them keep it to themselves because they don't want to appear guilty. I guess I can't blame them. Few people want to be involved in a murder case.

I put on my noise-canceling headphones, trying to block out the noise in the main room. I don't have my own office, only the higher ups do, and this desk is not the most ideal workspace. I glance at my desk, which is cluttered with case files. I open my laptop, making the most of it and focus on the task at hand, piecing together the paltry amount of evidence.

I spread the magazines out on my desk and flip open the first one, finding the article about Emilia's beach body. It details her recent weight loss and how great she looks now in her white and yellow striped bikini. She looked perfectly fine before, but I know what Hollywood beauty standards are like, unforgiving.

Her day on set mostly details how nice her trailer looks, how well she gets along with the cast and crew, and how she runs a few miles before coming to set. It doesn't reveal much except that she seems well-liked and has an affinity for fitness.

I check some articles online and find a recent one about how stars are just like us followed by a picture of her shopping at Whole Foods in West Hollywood two days ago. With the picture and the whole article about her new body, I can tell that she's not pregnant. No one can find out a person's pregnancy faster than the tabloids, so there would've already been rumors if anyone suspected anything.

I even type in "Emilia Cruz pregnant" into

Google, and nothing pops up. No speculations. So, a baby wasn't taken out of her when she was sliced open. That still leaves the question of why she was cut open in the first place.

I sigh and slump back in my chair, peering up at the ceiling. I don't like feeling stumped, but I am drawn to a challenge. So, I sit back up and look at the latest mentions of Emilia Cruz on Twitter, finally spotting something that I can work with.

The Screen Actors Guild Awards were last night, and she attended even though she wasn't nominated. I find a few pictures of her on the red carpet and click a link leading to her Instagram page. To my delight, she's fairly active.

In fact, there's a picture from last night!

She attended an after party at the W Hotel in Hollywood. The picture is a selfie of her as she beams at the camera with a party happening in the background. She looked so happy, totally unaware of what was about to happen next.

I click away from the photo, feeling the acidity from the coffee threatening to rise up in my throat. I decide to follow the one lead I have and look up the hotel's address. It looks like I won't be crammed in this stuffy station for the rest of the day.

Right now, I need to get to that hotel and see if I can dig up any other information. The last person she saw there was probably the person who did it.

My eyes shift to the clock on the bottom right of my screen. It's already 2:50.

"Oh, no," I mutter as I bury my face in my hands.

Even if he won't outwardly show it, Luke is going to be pissed. I grab my phone and type out a quick message.

I won't make it to the cake tasting. I'm really sorry but I have to go to West Hollywood for this case right now.

With guilt weighing down on my shoulder, I drop my empty coffee cup in the trash and grab my things, hoping that I'm not chasing a dead-end lead.

6

Kaitlyn

I battle afternoon traffic on Hollywood Boulevard to get to the W Hotel, a few horns blaring in the distance as I hunt down a parking spot. I step out of my car, being greeted with the signature Los Angeles smells of exhaust and jasmine. I can already see some of the white flowers down the sidewalk.

The W Hotel is a flashy, towering, white building right on the lively streets of the famous Hollywood Boulevard, next to all the main tourist attractions. I head into the lobby and take the guest lifts to the rooftop toward the check in desk. With stunning views of the Hollywood Hills, I walk past the bar, weaving in between the lounge chairs and toward the smiling middle-aged man in a dark suit.

"Detective Carr," I say as I show him my badge. "Are you the manager?"

"I am. I'm Mr. David Tapp, how can I help you?" he asks, the smile on his face quickly disappearing.

"There was a SAG Awards after party here last night. What can you tell me about it?"

Tapp shrugs and looks at me blankly.

"It started around 10:30 and ended around two in the morning, but some guests stayed for the night. If they decided to take the party back to their rooms, I wouldn't know."

"Did anything out of the ordinary happen?" I ask. Emilia posted her photo on Instagram right before midnight, so I know she was there at least around that time. But did she stay the whole time or leave early?

Tapp shakes his head.

"Can't think of anything. I don't closely monitor guests like that."

My eye threatens to twitch as I detect a bit of snootiness in his tone. I really don't need him getting difficult with me when I'm trying to find a murderer.

"Emilia Cruz attended the party last night. Do you know of her?" I ask.

"No, don't know her," Tapp replies.

I withhold a scoff as I dig my phone out of my pocket. I pull up a recent picture of her taken on the red carpet.

"This woman. She's an actress on *Quantum Frontier*," I tell him, trying to jog his memory. Most people have at least heard of her or recognize her face at this point.

Tapp shrugs.

"A lot of pretty blondes come through this hotel. It's hard to tell them apart. Is there anything else you need, Detective?" he asks in a pointed tone like he's trying to get rid of me.

Whether he wants to or not, he's going to have to work with me. There's evidence somewhere in here, and I'm going to find it.

"I need access to the staff who we were working last night and the security footage as well," I tell him. If anyone claims not to know anything, the cameras don't lie.

Tapp gives me a plastic smile.

"There should be enough paparazzi photos and social media posts for you to sift through. That should be all the media you need," he replies in a dismissive tone. "Besides, my staff was up working late. Most are off today, so you'll either have to wait for them to come in tomorrow or try to find them at their places of residence."

I can't legally demand for him to give up their names or addresses. I'll just have to convince him to change his mind. I doubt I have enough to force his hand by getting a subpoena. Before I can say another word, my phone rings. When I look at the screen, I see that it's Luke.

"I'll be right back," I walk a few feet away from the front desk to answer. "Hello?"

"Where exactly in West Hollywood are you?" Luke asks, the annoyance evident in his voice.

"Um… the W Hotel," I reply.

"I'll meet you there. I'm a few minutes away."

Before I can tell him that I'm in the middle of something, he hangs up. I hold my finger up to Tapp to let him know that I'll be a minute before walking out of the hotel and onto the sidewalk. I look up and down the street until I see a familiar Dodge Challenger pulling into a parking spot.

I'm in for it now.

Luke heads over to me with a white box in his hands, his eyes slightly narrowed.

"I didn't want to decide without you, so I

brought the last two contenders," he states as he opens the box to show me two pieces of cake.

I give him a sincerely apologetic look, knowing that I hurt his feelings by not showing up.

"I'm sorry. I tried to let you know that I couldn't make it."

"Last minute," he replies. "I wouldn't mind a little more warning next time."

My cheeks feel hot as I blush and lower my gaze to the cakes. Things just get away from me when I'm on the job.

"What kind do you have there?" I ask, wanting to help him choose between the last two. It's our wedding cake, a special piece of our special day.

"Strawberry Champagne and chocolate lavender," Luke replies as he hands me a fork.

I take a bite of each, thinking over my decision for a minute. I want to pick the right one, especially since I dropped the ball today.

"I like the chocolate lavender the most," I tell him, offering him a small smile.

Luke wrinkles his nose as he shuts the box.

"I think the strawberry Champagne is better. Since you didn't show up, we're going with my choice," he says before cracking a smile.

I laugh softly and step closer, wrapping my arms around his neck to press a soft kiss against his lips. The guilt starts to melt away slightly, and I'm grateful for his good attitude. I don't think anyone less laidback than him could deal with me. I need to get myself together before I end up losing the one person who truly gets me.

Once we break apart, Luke glances up at the hotel.

"An expensive place to have an affair," he teases me with a chuckle.

I playfully roll my eyes at him.

"Did you hear? Emilia Cruz was murdered."

Luke frowns and nods.

"Yeah, I heard. This is a huge case, Kaitlyn," he says.

"I got this," I assure him. "I'm following a lead here at the hotel."

Luke smiles and rubs my upper arm.

"I know you do," he replies. "If anyone can solve this case, it's you."

The amount of belief he has in me warms my heart. There have been plenty of instances when people have doubted my abilities, including my own mom when my little sister,

Violet, disappeared, I swear I saw the hope fade away in my mom's eyes as the days went on. I know she reached a point when she didn't believe in me.

But I found Violet and rescued her. I did that. And maybe I don't need to prove anything to anyone, but I'm still going to work hard like I always do.

"I love you," I whisper. I forgot to tell him this morning when I was rushing out the door.

"I love you, too." Luke says, pressing one more lingering kiss against my lips before drawing away. "I'll let you get back to it. I'm going to tell the baker that we've made our decision."

"We? Our decision?" I ask with a smirk.

Luke chuckles and heads back to his car.

I wave as he drives off, my mind immediately shifting gears. One wedding planning task is crossed off the list, which means I can focus on this case again. I hurry back into the hotel, not missing the sigh that Tapp lets out when he sees me.

"I'm going to be straight with you, Mr. Tapp. This is a murder case, and the victim was at that party. She was a young woman, an innocent victim, and all I'm trying to do is get justice for her and her family. Your security footage can help me trace her last steps and hopefully find the suspect. Now, will you help me?"

Tapp stares at me for a few seconds before picking up his desk phone and dialing an extension.

"Send the head of security to the lobby," he says.

7

Emilia

"Lift your chin, Ms. Cruz."

I tilted my head back as Olivia, my makeup artist, brushed dramatic eyeshadow above my eyelid. Admittedly, it was hard to stay still as the start of the SAG Awards steadily approached. I wasn't nominated for a category this year, but a lot of my friends were attending, and *Quantum Frontier* was nominated.

"Are you excited for tonight?" Olivia asked as she worked on my eyeliner, applying a subtle wing to highlight my blue eyes. She used the ring light on a flexible arm that was part of her travel kit to see her work more clearly, not messing up a single line or stroke of a brush. Her hair had been wrapped up into a tight bun, keeping it out of her face while she worked.

"Oh, yeah. Ever since I was little, I've wanted to come to this award show," I say, an eager smile crossing my lips.

"Well, from what I've seen on *Quantum Frontier*, I have no doubt that you'll be nominated next year," Olivia assured me as she gave me a warm look. She picked up a dark red lipstick and applied it carefully to my lips. "But you'll still turn heads *this* year."

My heart automatically skipped a beat at the thought. It was hard to process all the attention I had been getting since I started starring in that show. How did a small-town girl from Iowa become a breakout Hollywood star? I couldn't believe my own luck.

I had worked hard to get to this point. Acting classes and coaches. Countless auditions. Hours spent on set. Finally, people were taking notice of all that work, and I wasn't planning on plateauing or fading back into the background. I was shooting for the stars.

"Done. Take a look," Olivia said with a proud look on her face.

I rose off the bench and peered at my reflection in the bathroom mirror. My face looked photoshopped, striking and beautiful. The lash extensions added to the drama but in a natural kind of way, accentuating and widening my normally small eyes.

"It's perfect," I say, flashing a smile.

Olivia clapped happily before unclipping my hair, letting the waves fall down my back. She gave it a gentle fluff and applied some more hairspray before stepping back to take another look at her work.

"Beautiful. Absolutely stunning."

A knock startled me.

"That must be your dress!" Olivia said before hurrying to the door.

"Ding dong! The dress is here!" Trinity Luvenier announced before walking inside, her black curls bouncing with each step. She hung the dress up on my closet door before unzipping the garment bag, revealing a beautiful, silver cocktail dress with a sequined exterior and thin straps.

My eyes widened in awe as I approached it, drifting my fingers along the shiny sequins. Tonight, I was going to look like Hollywood royalty, which was something I hadn't been sure if I would ever achieve or not. All of my dreams were coming true.

"I love it!" I exclaimed, itching to get it on.

Trinity and Olivia helped me change into the dress without messing up my hair and make-up. Once Trinity zipped me up, she stepped back and let me take another look at myself in the tall mirror next to the closet.

"They're going to be all over you tonight," Trinity told me, sharing a pleased look with Olivia.

"I'm ready," I said gazing at this new version of myself.

I hardly recognized the girl I used to be. I was becoming the person the younger version of me always dreamed of, and that meant I was doing something right. When my phone started to vibrate, I grabbed it off the bed and saw my mom's face.

Trinity and Olivia waved good-bye and told me to text if I needed anything else before shutting the door and leaving me alone in the room.

"Hey, Mom," I greeted her with a smile.

"Oh my gosh! You look beautiful, honey!" my mom exclaimed as her beaming face filled the screen.

Lately, there had been a lot of this; calls, texts, and FaceTime. I was so busy on set that it was hard to find time to visit her at home.

She was born and had lived her whole life in a small Iowa farming town, the place where I grew up. Right now, we looked totally different with my glammed-up look and her casual attire of an oversized white T-shirt over her plump body. Her blonde hair was short and straight, while mine was long and fixed into waves. She probably put some Carmex on her lips, while mine were adorned with expensive lipstick.

"Oh, I miss you, Sarah. It feels like I haven't seen you in forever," Mom sighed.

I hadn't heard my birth name in a long time. At this point, I *was* Emilia Cruz, even to myself.

"I miss you too," I told her. "The SAG Awards are about to start."

"I can't wait to see the photos!" my mom replied cheerfully. She had always been my biggest supporter, taking me to acting classes and auditions before I graduated college and moved out to Los Angeles. She was nervous for me, but she never asked me to stay in Iowa where there was nothing for me but family.

"What's been going on at home? Anything happening?" I asked. I knew she felt lonely without me there, so, I encouraged her to talk about the little, daily things that came up. It seemed to make her feel better.

My mom's eyebrows knitted together for a second as she thought.

"There was something I was going to tell you... oh! You won't believe who I ran into at the Hy-Vee the other day."

"Who?" I asked. Hy-Vee is a grocery store chain popular in the Midwest. Mom was always meeting and catching up with people from town. She was a social butterfly if ever there was one.

"Colin Kapowski's mom, Ellen!"

My blood ran cold at the sound of my ex-boyfriend's name. We had been together for years, in high school and then college. Everyone expected us to get married.

"Oh, I remember how cute you two were together!"

My jaw clenched as I listened to her fawn over someone she didn't even truly know. He was an All-American baseball player at Iowa State and that's all he would ever be to people back home. A local kid who did well for himself. But all of that was just a cover-up for who he is deep down inside, and unfortunately, I saw the ugly side of him. I wouldn't ever forget that.

"Oh," I merely said, not wanting to talk about him.

"He's a real nice boy. A true gentleman! Probably far more serious and selfless than those L.A. pretty boys," my mom scoffed. She knew nothing of who he really was.

Her face then brightened up. "Maybe you can reconnect with him. I'm sure I can get his number from Ellen."

My heart hammered in my chest as I shook my head, not wanting to ever hear his voice again.

"I have to go, Mom," I told her, watching her face drop. She didn't mean to upset me, she didn't know what had happened. But I just couldn't deal with this right now. I needed to have a clear head before all of those cameras were pointed at me.

"Oh, okay. Call me soon? I want to hear about how much fun you have at the show," my mom said with a hopeful look in her eyes.

"I will. Love you," I said, my chest aching at the sound of her voice.

All she did was try to support me, but I wished that she didn't think so highly of Colin. Even L.A. douchebags were better than him.

"Love you, honey."

I hung up the call and dropped my phone on the bed, closing my eyes and collecting myself. I couldn't be Sarah Matthews, the girl who had her heart smashed to pieces and her trust betrayed. I had to be Emilia Cruz, the actress with promise. No other version of myself would survive out here and all I was trying to do was fight to stay alive.

8

Kaitlyn

Footage fills multiple monitors as I stand in the cramped, darkened room with Paul Ternitzky, the hotel's head of security who wears too much cologne and has a ring of orange dust around his mouth. There's an empty Cheetos bag next to his Coke can, which seems to be the culprit. The security room is packed full of audiovisual equipment and plenty of screens that show nearly every corner and hallway of the hotel. There's a whole timeline that I have to cover, and I hope that the footage all of this fancy equipment captured can fill in some gaps for me. If Emilia made a move, I want to be able to track it.

"The party was in the main ballroom," Ternitzky tells me as he pulls up the camera footage focused on the middle of the large room. “What time do you want to go back to?”

“Beginning of the party. I want to see if she arrives with anyone,” I say as I cross my arms over my chest, watching him scroll back through the footage to around ten o’clock last night. I lean closer to the main screen that he’s pulled the video up on, watching the ballroom steadily fill with people in ball gowns and suits.

Around 10:45, the familiar blonde woman waltzes into frame, easily recognizable in that shimmery dress. Emilia approaches a server walking around with a tray of Champagne glasses and takes one before glancing around like she’s trying to figure out what to do.

“There she is,” I point, hoping that Ternitzky will keep an eye out for her as well. The camera quality is decent, but as more and more people pile into the room, it starts to get harder to keep track of her.

Ternitzky speeds through parts of the footage at my direction, stopping when I say so that I can trace her movements. For the most part, Emilia doesn’t do anything out of the ordinary. She makes the rounds, talking to a few people and moving amongst constantly shifting knots of conversation.

"Wait… is that you?" I ask Ternitzky as I point to a large, muscular man with a shaved head that comes into the camera's view.

Ternitzky gives me a bit of a sheepish look as he nods.

"I went over to make sure everyone was doing fine. I used to be on the force, so it's hard to just sit behind a screen all day."

I nod my understanding. I get antsy sitting behind a desk too, which is why I often find any excuse to be out of the station.

"Anything catch your eye while you were there?"

Ternitzky rubs the back of his neck as he shrugs.

"Not really. Just a bunch of rich people talking about how amazing their lives are," he says. "I'll admit that I wasn't only there to check on everyone. I've been working on a screenplay, so it seemed like a good chance to meet and network with some of the directors that were in attendance."

This town is full of mythical stories of waiters getting their breakout roles by serving influential producers and security guards getting their scripts optioned from a chance meeting at a bar.

"Skip ahead a little," I say as Emilia still continues to sway on the screen with her made-for-TV smile.

As I watch the security footage of the party, my eyes are fixed to Emilia. Her stunning silver gown hugs her slim figure, and she looks even thinner than she did in the show.

Her long blonde hair falls in loose waves down her back, and I notice that she seems tense, or perhaps a bit guarded. Although it is hard to be sure from the angle of the camera, it looks as though her demeanor has changed from nervousness to something more serious. I wonder if something is troubling her, or if she's simply overwhelmed with the excitement of the party.

As I continue to watch, I see that Emilia keeps glancing around the room, as if searching for someone or something. Her movements are graceful and elegant, but there is an undercurrent of tension that I can't quite put my finger on.

Despite my concerns, I can't deny that Emilia looks absolutely stunning in her gown. Her beauty is only enhanced by the shimmering fabric, and I can't help but feel a twinge of envy as I watch her move through the crowd with effortless grace.

As the party wears on, I find myself wondering what might be going on beneath the surface. Is there something troubling Emilia? Or am I simply reading too much into her demeanor?

Then, Emilia steps out of frame and disappears.

"Did she leave? Go to the hallway camera," I tell Ternitzky as my eyebrows furrow. The party is far from over. Did she just have to go to the restroom?

Ternitzky shows me the hallway camera outside of the ballroom. Emilia wanders down the hallway and goes around the corner. He brings up the closest camera, but it only shows the beginning of the next hallway, from which Emilia quickly slips out of view.

"Where is she going? It doesn't even look like she's heading toward the foyer. Unless she's taking the long way around," I mutter as Ternitzky tries to find another camera view of her.

"I don't know. She should've come into this hallway, but I've skimmed through this camera footage for fifteen minutes. It's like she disappeared," Ternitzky sighs in frustration as he continues pulling up multiple camera angles.

I lean back as my jaw tenses. Granted, some of the angles are poorly set up, missing some corners and only showing part of the entrances.

"There are a few serious blind spots in this camera set up. Who would know about the location of the cameras besides you?"

"Anyone who has access to the footage or knows the layout of the cameras," Ternitzky says, looking at me. "I see where you're headed, but I don't know. That'd take some serious planning, and it is more likely just a coincidence."

"Can you give me a list of people who have access to this room or who know about these blind spots?"

I want to hit every mark. I don't know if Emilia just got lucky sneaking past all those cameras or someone directed her, but I'm going to figure it out one way or another.

"That could be almost any employee. All they would need to do would be to look up and make a note of where the cameras were. They aren't exactly hidden. But, I'll get you the list if you want to try to run that down, of course. Is there anything else you need?"

"Copies of the party footage and the outside

hallway from when the party starts to when it ends. I'm going to see if the front desk receptionist is around."

Ternitzky checks his silver watch.

"Her name is Tori Nguyen. She should be back from break now," he says. "I'll start making those copies."

I pat Ternitzky on the shoulder briefly, out of gratitude, before leaving the security room, my eyes sweeping the hallway. Grey carpeting, white walls, and golden lights direct me up ahead. It seems so ordinary, and I wonder if Emilia happened to come down this way.

As I search for someone, questions flood my mind in an unending loop. Did she use a back or emergency exit, or did she leave through the lobby and front door? Surely, someone must have seen her.

I ponder the possibility that she had a companion who distracted any witnesses, allowing her to slip away unnoticed. Who could this accomplice be? A friend, family member, or colleague?

9

Kaitlyn

Before heading straight to the receptionist's desk in the lobby, I venture to the main ballroom where the party was held. I don't expect to find anything obvious, but I want to see the space for myself. I open the wooden double doors and step inside, getting a good look at the large space that's now filled with rows of chairs for a conference happening soon.

All I know is that Emilia didn't return to the party after leaving. That doesn't sound like a bathroom break or stepping out for some air. She left for some reason, even if things seemed to be going well. However, the cameras didn't capture any audio, so who knows what else could have happened?

I walk back out into the hallway, locating the

camera mounted on the wall that points toward the ballroom. I thought I'd get more information from the footage, but when are things ever that easy? I will have to rely on what I can get out of interviews.

As a detective, I've learned that witnesses can be unreliable. Even though TV shows and movies often depict eyewitness testimony as infallible, the truth is that memories can be altered by a variety of factors.

I've seen cases where multiple witnesses have given conflicting accounts of what happened, each one convinced that their version of events is the correct one. And it's not a matter of intentional deception - people's perceptions and memories can be influenced by emotion, bias, and even suggestion.

This is why it's important to corroborate witness accounts and consider multiple perspectives when trying to piece together what really happened. One person's recollection of events may not necessarily be the whole truth, and it's crucial to be aware of this when conducting an investigation.

Furthermore, even firsthand experiences can be unreliable. That's why it's important to approach eyewitness testimony with a healthy dose of skepticism, and to seek out additional evidence and testimony to support or refute the claims made by witnesses.

Heading toward the lobby, I feel a sense of relief at the sight when I see someone other than David Tapp at the front desk.

"There was a party last night. Have you heard or seen anything about this woman? Her name is Emilia Cruz," I ask.

She leans closer and peers at the photo for a second before shaking her head. Her bun is so tightly fixed on top of her head that it doesn't even shift.

"I'm sorry. I wasn't here last night. Did something happen?"

Before I can respond, I hear a yawn behind me.

"I'm never working the late shift ever again," the young, dark-haired woman in a black business suit mutters to herself as she heads toward the bar, hastily tying her long hair into a low ponytail.

"Did you work last night?"

She eyes me suspiciously with heavy-lidded eyes, thrown off-guard by my question.

"Yeah, why?" she replies.

I show her my badge.

"I'm Detective Carr. Do you mind if I ask you a few questions?" I say as I gesture to the seats behind us, hoping that she can tell me anything at all.

Clearly exhausted, she doesn't seem all that enthusiastic about being questioned but she doesn't argue. Wordlessly, she goes over to one of the lounge chairs and slumps into it.

I sit next to her, angling my body to face her.

"What's your name?" I start off.

"Jane… Jane Patel," she says, her fingertips sinking into the cushioned arms of the chair. "I tend bar."

"What was last night's party like?"

She shrugs.

"Bunch of Hollywood types. They mostly had their drinks in the ballroom, but a few came over here for some peace and quiet."

I show her Emilia's picture.

"What about her?"

"Yeah, she didn't come get a drink, though," she says quickly. "I was heading to the break room when I saw her and some guy arguing by the ice machine."

"Did you hear what they were saying?"

Jane shakes her head, no.

"I didn't want to get involved. I just went

right to the break room. By the time I left, they were gone."

It's not the end of the world that she doesn't know what they were talking about. What I'm more concerned about is *who* Emilia was arguing with.

"I need you to help me figure out who she was with. Did you get a good look at the guy?" I say as I open Emilia's Instagram.

"Yeah, I actually think I've seen him on TV. I just don't know his name," Jane says, her eyes narrowing. "He's some older guy. Like late 40's or 50's."

Every little detail she gives me nudges me in the right direction, and I'm relieved to finally have an eyewitness who can give me some information.

"Do you see him in any of these photos?" I ask as I scroll through Emilia's social media.

Jane doesn't say anything at first and then she points at a photo of Emilia standing next to an older man with thinning dark hair, slim figure, and thin-framed glasses over his blue eyes. They're both smiling with their arms around each other.

After getting Jane's contact info, I let her go and continue to click around, quickly finding out that the man is Richard M. Murphy. Not only is he an old child actor, but he's also the director of *Quantum Frontier*.

The argument, of course, could be nothing at all, but the fact that it happened right before her death is significant.

I feel a rush of excitement as I realize I have my next lead. I know I need to question Richard and find out what he and Emilia talked about last night. This could be a crucial piece of information that ties into her murder.

Walking out of the hotel, my mind is racing. I can't help but feel a sense of triumph at having made progress on the case. It's a small victory, but in a world where so much seems uncertain and unpredictable, any victory feels important.

But even as I bask in this sense of accomplishment, I can't shake the unnerving pressure that is weighing down on me. Who knows if there is true justice in this world? It's a question that has plagued philosophers and thinkers for centuries. Some believe that justice is a universal concept, rooted in the very fabric of reality.

Others believe that it's a human construct, a set of norms and values that we have created to help us navigate the complexities of society.

Regardless of one's perspective, the reality is that we live in a world where tragedy can strike at any moment. It's a reality that can be difficult to come to terms with, but it's also what drives us to fight for justice and to seek truth and meaning in the face of adversity.

As I contemplate these weighty questions, I know that my duty as a detective is to continue pursuing the truth, no matter how difficult or elusive it may be. It's a daunting task, but it's one that I am committed to seeing through to the end. For, in a world where justice can seem so uncertain, the pursuit of truth is a noble and worthy endeavor.

10

Kaitlyn

I walk up to the police station, and it's as if I have come home. The building is a blur of beige walls, yellowed linoleum floors, and chaotic bulletin boards. A slight breeze through the door makes fliers rustle and move, catching my eye. The air smells like coffee and heavy duty cleaning supplies. As my feet shuffle along the floor, I pass a faded sign shadowed by a blue-tipped lamp that reads "No weapons allowed past this point."

It doesn't take me long to find Captain Medvil. It's like he's been waiting for me, leaning against the front desk with a Big Gulp in his hand. Evident by his bigger size under his slightly strained, white button-down shirt, he loves enjoying his soda in the afternoons. There are noticeable lines on his face and bags under his eyes as he approaches his mid-fifties, and he's definitely worn down from years in this demanding job.

I can still rely on him, though it won't be long until he retires; he's been counting down the days. After hundreds of cases, he's ready to hand over the reins to someone else.

I walk up to Captain Medvil, my excitement clearly evident. He nods in acknowledgement.

"Any leads?" he asks, his eyes fixed on me.

I stop in front of him and show him a picture of the director of *Quantum Frontier*.

"This is Richard Murphy," I say. "He was seen arguing with Emilia at the hotel before she left. I want to follow up with him and see what they were arguing about."

Captain Medvil inspects the photo carefully before nodding in agreement. He sets his Big Gulp down on the front desk and crosses his arms over his broad chest, his expression serious.

"As you can imagine, this case is getting a lot of attention. The press has been blowing up our phones."

I nod in agreement. Hollywood stars are used to being in the limelight, but a murder case brings a whole new level of attention. People are hungry for details, no matter how gruesome. In fact, that only makes the story more interesting.

Despite the pressure and the constant demand for information, I remain focused on my duty to find the person who did this. I know that every lead I follow and every piece of evidence I uncover brings me one step closer to the truth. And that, in the end, is what matters most.

"Of course. I'll tell them I have no comment."

The press has to be carefully manipulated, otherwise they will disclose too much to the general public and blow the case in court, if it ever even gets there).

Captain Medvil sighs.

"Because this case is so huge, we need more investigators working it other than you," he says.

My gaze hardens, my jaw tenses. I don't like the sound of that. Does he doubt me and my abilities to get this case solved?

"With all due respect, Captain… I can handle this case by myself. Adding someone else into the mix will just slow me down," I say, keeping my voice level and steady, despite wanting to yell. I don't like feeling doubted in the slightest, not after busting my ass so much. No lead investigator does.

Now, it's his turn to give me a stern look.

"I'm not asking, Detective," Captain Medvil replies in a firm voice, his gaze unwavering. "I'm telling you that you will have a partner, and I've already selected her." With that, he leads me towards the rows of desks half-filled with officers.

As we approach one particular one, Captain Medvil stops in front of an African American woman who looks to be in her late thirties. She is focused intently on some paperwork, but looks up as we approach. A framed picture of two teenagers - a boy and a girl - sits on her desk.

"This is Tracie Freeman," Captain Medvil says, introducing us.

I take a closer look at Tracie, trying to gauge what kind of partner she might be. I don't know much about her, so I can't help but wonder why Captain Medvil thinks she's the right person to assist me with this case.

"Hello," she says as she rises to her feet,

holding out her hand. She has a pleasant demeanor, eager smile, dark brown skin and intense eyes that seem to penetrate my very being.

I nod and shake her hand, caught off guard by her iron grip. Our eyes meet, and there is seriousness written all over her face. She isn't here to mess around, which I suppose is a good thing.

"Have you worked homicide before?"

Tracie nods.

"I have. A few cases actually. I went to the academy later than most, but I'm just as capable as anyone else here to handle this case."

I'll have to see how she is in the field. I don't necessarily want to doubt her, but this case is important. I'm on a roll right now, and I don't want to lose my momentum by having to babysit anyone. I could be on the way to meet Richard now, but I have to get her caught up first.

"I'm following a lead right now that I guess you can assist me with. You are familiar with the Emilia Cruz case?" I wait for her to nod before I continue. "Emilia was seen arguing with her director at the hotel before she left. I want to talk to him."

I'm keenly aware of the fact that Captain Medvil is standing next to me, watching my every move. I have to admit that I'm being a lot more personable than perhaps I would be otherwise.

Tracie's eyebrows lift slightly.

"Richard Murphy," she says. "He had a lot riding on that show."

"Oh, you know about him?" I ask.

Tracie nods, her expression not wavering.

"I did a lot of research once Captain put me on the case. I'd prefer to get started now. If there's anything else you need to catch me up on, we can discuss it in the car."

My eyes dart over to Captain Medvil, who walks away before I can pull him aside for a private conversation about this partner that he's chosen for me. No matter how much research she's done, this is still *my* case.

"Let's go. Richard's house is a decent drive away," I say as I head toward the exit.

"Shouldn't we contact Mr. Murphy first?" Tracie asks as she hurries to gather her stuff and catch up.

"No." I push open the door and head out to my car, not slowing my pace.

Once I get into the driver's seat, I check my

phone to see a new email from Paul Ternitzky. It must be the hotel footage I asked for. "There's some hotel footage you can look over later."

"You already had them release the footage? You didn't get a warrant for it first?" Tracie questions me once she gets in the passenger's seat.

She's the type to do everything by the book. There's nothing wrong with following the rules, but when time is of the essence, I have to move things along a little bit faster than what the rules suggest.

"No need. We have no obligation to get a search warrant because we already have permission from the owner."

"But you do know that the permission can be revoked at any point, right? The search warrant should be our top priority."

I clench my jaw. She isn't wrong.

Maybe I was a bit pushy about getting the footage, but I didn't want anyone standing in my way.

"Let's talk to this guy and then we'll file the paperwork," I tell her, my eyes shifting to hers.

Tracie stares for a few moments. It's only been about ten minutes, and we've butted heads more than once already.

"Okay, let's go," she says as she turns forward with a determined look on her face.

I wrap my fingers around the steering wheel in a tight grip. I suppose having someone like her is better than having someone who doesn't care.

11

Kaitlyn

My knuckles rap against the dark wood of Richard's triple glass-paneled front door. A light wind rustles the spiny fronds of nearby palm trees as the sound of traffic hums in the distance. Overall, it's a nice, quiet neighborhood full of Spanish style houses. Richard's house is no exception - the bright white exterior is complemented by a lush green lawn, making for an eye-catching display.

As I step inside, my gaze is drawn to the mosaic-styled entry rug beneath my feet. The intricate patterns and bright colors are overwhelming, almost dizzying in their complexity.

After a few moments, the door opens, and the man from Emilia's Instagram peers at us with a confused look on his face. His eyes are slightly red, and it seems like he's still wearing his pajamas: a loose-fitting white t-shirt and black and blue plaid pants.

"Yes?" he asks, sounding drained.

When Tracie and I show our badges, his shoulders drop.

"I'm Detective Carr. This is Detective Freeman. We'd like to ask you a few questions about last night."

Richard sighs as he leans against the doorframe, seemingly the only thing keeping him upright.

"I'm guessing this is about Emilia. About… what happened to her," he murmurs, his throat tight.

"Yes, sir. May we come in? It may be best if you sit down," Tracie suggests.

Richard sucks in a deep breath before nodding and leading me into his house. It looks more lived-in than I would have thought from the outside. The wood floor isn't recently polished, and there are little things scattered all over the place. The smell of coffee lingers in the air as he guides us into his open living room, sunlight pouring through the glass door that leads out to his porch. He nearly collapses into his leather loveseat, gesturing to the matching couch.

Tracie and I take a seat, tension hanging in the air. He's certainly upset, but that could be for two very different reasons. He either truly cares about Emilia and is in a state of grief and shock, or he's riddled with guilt over having a part in her death and is scared about the consequences.

"You attended the after party at the W last night. Emilia was there too."

Richard lifts his eyes to mine and nods, a distant look filling his face.

"Yes. We went together with some of the other cast members."

Together. I eye him for a moment, taking in how distraught he is over her death. Of course, it's tragic, but I have to look past the surface. He's about twenty years older than her and probably only really knew her once she got the role for his show. Maybe there's something more to their relationship than just a professional one.

"Are you married, Richard?" I ask.

Richard's eyebrows rise slightly with confusion.

"Um… yes," he says.

Tracie suddenly stands and grabs a picture

frame off the entertainment stand, showing it to me and him.

"These are your kids?" she asks. It seems like she already knows what angle I'm working.

Richard nods.

I rest my elbows on my legs as I lean closer to him.

"How would you describe the nature of your relationship with Emilia?" I ask.

Richard scoffs a little and shakes his head.

"I wasn't having an affair with her if that's what you're getting at," he states firmly. "She was a friend. A good one."

I glance over at Tracie, who nods subtly before she sits back down and takes out a notepad and pen. I want to ask about the argument but I need to take my time and make him comfortable first.

"When did you first meet Emilia?" I ask.

Richard thinks for a moment.

"A while ago at some actors showcase. I was looking for fresh talent for my upcoming show, *Quantum Frontier*. She did a few scenes, and I knew that I wanted to work with her. She was a natural, you know? Emotional and smart."

She is pretty good in the show, I think.

"And where did things go from there?" Tracie hops in.

"I told her about my show, which I had been working on for years. It was my dream project to bring to fruition, and I wanted her to audition for the female lead," Richard says, moving his hands restlessly as he speaks. "But I'm not the only one who took an interest in her at the showcase. Some casting director for a popular soap opera offered her a higher paying role than what I could initially afford."

"She didn't take it?"

Richard smiles slightly in a bittersweet manner as he shakes his head.

"No, she didn't. She believed in my idea before anyone else, and when it got approved, I gave her the lead part. Since she was pretty new to the scene, I took her under my wing. Like as a mentor."

"In what way?" Tracie asks. "How did you mentor her?"

Richard shrugs.

"I gave her advice on how to network and develop her skills. She also came to me about scripts she got for movies she could do when we were on hiatus."

I stare at him blankly.

"That's when we are off. In between seasons. It's common for actors to take on other work especially if they have a hit show and want to do something that would get them noticed. I wanted her to be successful. She was on the path to that for a while," he says before a dark shadow seemed to pass over his face. "Until a few months ago. Things started to change."

That doesn't sound good.

"Go on," I say.

Richard sighs and leans back in his seat, staring ahead.

"She just… started to move away; became more distant and less engaged personally and professionally. She started to get to the set late. It was like she wasn't even there half the time. I knew something was wrong. Initially, I thought it was drugs or something."

"Did something change in her life? A break-up? Fallout with family?" Tracie asks.

"She's close with her mom, and she wasn't dating anyone. I would have heard about that, I'm sure. What changed is she started following this absurd, new diet that made her lose a lot of weight. Too much weight in a very small amount of time. She would get dizzy and look like she was about to pass out." Richard shakes his head.

"Do you know if that diet has a specific name? Or if someone she knew recommended it?" I ask.

Richard laughs in a cold, humorless manner.

"At one point, she said that if she became enlightened enough, she could live off air. They were feeding her nonsense and it was slowly killing her."

"Sounds like some sort of cult," Tracie says.

"What about last night? Didn't you have an argument?" I ask.

Richard's eyes widen slightly. He must've not expected us to know about that. A frown crosses his face as he nods.

"It was… stupid. I offered her a finger sandwich, and she turned her nose up, saying it wasn't part of her new diet. She hardly eats anything at all, and I was just sick and tired of seeing her do that to herself. I stormed off to get some air. I guess she followed me, and we argued more. She told me to stay out of her business."

"She seems very invested in this new lifestyle," Tracie comments.

"You need to look into that," Richard says. "I don't know what happened to her after she left the hotel, but whoever she had started associating with clearly didn't have her best interests at heart."

"Thank you for your time, Richard. We'll be in touch," I say rising to my feet.

Richard walks us out, a somber look haunting his face as he watches us get in my car.

"We're going to her place now, right?" Tracie asks me as she looks over the notes. I flash a smile. That's exactly what I was thinking.

"Yep. I don't know if this diet has anything to do with her death, but it's a good start."

"That's all that matters," Tracie underlines something.

When I pull away, the heavy thud of my heartbeat echoes in my head.

12

Kaitlyn

A few calls, some paperwork and we get a search warrant that gives us access to Emilia's apartment, which is located on the top floor of a midrise building in West Hollywood. We take the elevator for a long ride upward, able to see the city growing smaller since the back wall is glass. As far as I know, she didn't make it home last night, but I hope there's still a clue or two about what could've happened.

I use the key we get from the super to unlock the front door of Emilia's apartment before pushing it open, revealing a tidy space.

The design is clearly modern and minimalist with stark, white walls and dark hardwood floors. The furniture looks new with sleek material, contemporary designs, and pops of bright color added in. To my right, there is an open kitchen with new appliances and a marble island in the center. The living room has plenty of sunlight from the floor-to-ceiling windows, which give an amazing view of the city.

"Nice place," I say as my eyes do a thorough sweep, trying to find anything out of the ordinary. At least it's clear that she doesn't have a pet waiting for her to never come home.

Tracie quietly does her own inspection of the living room, peering at some novels on the coffee table.

I wander into the hallway to my right, seeing three doors. I pop into the laundry room and bathroom, but the place I'm most interested in is her bedroom at the end of the hallway. I glance around, taking in the sight of a kind-sized bed with linen sheets and a walk-in closet. What really catches my eye is her desk near the two large windows in her room, light spilling onto a closed laptop.

Bingo.

I sit at her desk and open her laptop. The home screen pops right up, showing a picture of her with her arm around her mom, both smiling from ear to ear. The cornfields in the background make me think that this might have been taken in Iowa. I wonder if a part of her missed her home.

If she knew what fate awaited her, would she still have moved to California to pursue her dream?

"Found the laptop!" I call out.

Tracie heads into the bedroom a few seconds later, looking over my shoulder at the home screen.

"It wasn't locked?" she asks.

I shake my head, no.

"I guess she didn't feel nervous about anyone looking through it. Or she wanted someone to."

I can't count anything out. I don't even know if there's anything here.

"Let's check her browser history," Tracie says.

I look through the folders on the desktop, which filled with multiple PDFs.

Diet Guidelines

Ritual Practices

Meeting Schedule

365 Day Transformation

Rules and Conditions

. . .

"Click that," Tracie points to a PDF document titled 'Welcome' that's toward the top of her files.

I open the file called *The Order of the Enlightened.*

I look through the document about what appears to be some sort of religion. The table of contents shows chapters discussing meditation, spiritual practice, and diet to help achieve new levels of being.

"It's certainly extreme," Tracie's eyebrows lift.

I close the document and start pulling up photos, my stomach starting to sink. They are pictures of Emilia attending retreats with the group, sitting in circles in the woods with their hands joined together. The women are different ethnicities, but all are young and attractive. A fire burns in the center of their circle, and they chant with wide, dilated eyes.

"It looks like they're high on something," I say as I gesture to their faces.

"But on what?" Tracie wonders.

I start looking through more documents, wanting to know more about these retreats.

Telling from all the pictures, Emilia had been a very active member in the last few months. She must've been hiding things well if the press didn't catch wind of this. All they knew was that she went on a diet.

"Enlightenment powder," I say, pointing to a line in the *Ritual Practices* document. "I don't know what it's made of or its origin, but it's probably illegal. Maybe a mixture of cocaine and something else?"

"How did she get roped into this?" Tracie sighs as she shakes her head.

"They found a weak spot," I say. All of these groups go after vulnerable people, promising things they can't deliver.

"Who is the leader?" Tracie asks as she leans closer to the screen to get a better look.

I scroll to the bottom to see a signature, but it just says, '*The Prophet*' and nothing else. It'll be easy to tell who's running this circus from the pictures, though. I pull a few of them up that show the group facing one man.

He's a bit older, probably in his forties, but he's also noticeably attractive like one of those charming soap opera stars. His brown hair is short but still covers his ears and comes down to the middle of his forehead above his blue eyes.

In every picture, he's wearing linen clothing and no shoes with a beaded necklace around his neck. If anyone is the leader, it's him.

"We need to figure out who he is."

Tracie takes a clear picture of his face and taps around on her phone.

"I'll have Vikram at the station look him up," she says.

Vikram Kumar is the guy we go to when we need data or information. He knows exactly where to look and how to dig stuff up. Most of the stuff comes from social media and he's pretty quick with the results. If there's anything to find, it could take him a week or so, which is faster than anyone else I've ever worked with. But today he sets a record.

Within five minutes, he sends a name back.

"Elijah Nova," Tracie reveals.

"How did he find that out so quickly?" I gasp.

"He's seen his ads and posts on Instagram," she gives me a wink.

I scoff a little, shaking my head, and we both laugh. Sometimes, you get lucky.

"Elijah Nova. Quite a fitting name," I mutter before shutting off the laptop and picking it up off the desk. There are too many pieces of information on it for me to leave it here. "Let's take this back to the station. We know what to look into next."

I open a new evidence bag and fill out the paperwork to preserve the chain of evidence.

Tracie pauses as she glances around Emilia's apartment. There are traces of her everywhere. An old Iowa college baseball hat hangs on a hook on her wall. A cedarwood candle sits on her nightstand. Some magazines with her featured on the front cover lie in the cubby of her desk.

At the end of the day, she was just a young woman with a goal. People commented on every aspect of her. Her body. Her face. Her acting. Her lifestyle.

Now, people are talking about her death. Fame is the death of peace.

"She was so young," Tracie says.

I don't have kids to worry about, but I have a feeling that she'll hug hers very tightly tonight. Our job shows us that life truly is fleeting. One moment, someone is on top of the world. The next moment, they're cut open on the medical examiner's table.

13

Kaitlyn

After logging the laptop into evidence and hopping onto my own computer, Tracie pulls a chair up to my desk. I'm already itching to leave the station and talk to someone connected to *The Order of the Enlightened*, but I need to know what I'm walking into first. For all I know, these people may be highly dangerous. One of their members has just been brutally murdered.

"Let's see if these people even exist on the Internet," I say, giving my fingers a quick flex before typing the group's name on Google.

"Everything exists on the Internet," Tracie smiles.

"Doesn't mean it's easy to find," I sigh as Google doesn't produce all that many results. I figured these guys would keep themselves low on the radar. Even if they fully believe in what they stand for, they know it's controversial and needs to be kept on the down low. Their exclusivity probably sucks more people in, too.

"My daughter says that everything is on that video app. What is it? TikTak?" Tracie asks.

I nearly snort, pinching the bridge of my nose to keep myself together. It's not like I'm really young and cool anymore. I'm in my early thirties, but I still know about TikTok.

"TikTok is probably a good place to start," I reply as I pull it up on my phone. I really don't go on it much, but Luke sends me so many videos that I just downloaded it so that I can watch them. Admittedly, there's some funny stuff on there. I never thought I'd use it for a murder investigation, though.

I type *The Order of the Enlightened* into the search bar, hoping that at least something shows up. To my delight, a few videos pop up from several different accounts. I click on the first and turn the volume up as a redhead woman around my age starts talking.

"Please don't scroll. If you're in the Los Angeles area, I need you to listen to me. My name is Hailey Lott. I'm a voice and motion capture actress in the video game industry. At the height of my career, *The Order of the Enlightened* sought me out and encouraged me to join them. You probably haven't heard of them before, but they're incredibly toxic and dangerous. If they ever approach you, do not join them! If you want to know more about my personal experiences, comment below."

I look over at Tracie, who is completely tuned in. We've hit a gold mine. If other people are already wanting to talk publicly, and they can attest to the practices of this group, it can help us understand what Emilia was going through. Maybe that can point to her killer.

I go to Hailey's profile and find her next video.

"Hey, guys. A lot of you wanted to know more about the Order. I was part of them for about half a year before I got out. During that time, they encouraged a lot of dangerous practices with the goal of achieving immortality. I know that sounds crazy, but I can't explain how they're able to get in people's heads. They just do. I was encouraged not to eat and to only have a relationship with the Prophet, the group's leader. I did what I was told until I couldn't take it anymore."

I look through a few other videos from other

people, but they mostly say the same thing. The Order is dangerous and crazy. The practices are questionable and toxic.

"I want to talk to Hailey. She knows more than what she put online," I say.

Tracie nods her agreement.

"I can find her contact information, and we can set up an interview time," she offers.

I shake my head and look up Hailey in the police database.

"No, find her address and we'll swing by her place and pay her a visit," I reply.

Tracie narrows her eyes slightly.

"Isn't it more professional to reach out? It's not like she's a suspect."

I turn to face her after writing down Hailey's address.

"Look, I know you're trying to be courteous, but we have to move fast. The killer may already be on the run. I don't give anyone a heads-up that I'm coming so that they can't give anyone a heads-up."

I can't give anyone a chance to run from me.

Tracie's expression remains still as she finally nods.

I know that I'm a bit more impulsive than she prefers, but I don't like to slow my pace and wait. Paperwork and clearance just give the killer more time to get away or cover up their tracks.

"Alright, let's go," I say heading out to my car.

Once she gets in, I turn on my GPS and let it lead me to Hailey's apartment building in downtown Los Angeles. I manage to find a parking spot on the street. As I step out of the car, fifteen stories of luxury apartments loom over me.

Tracie and I go through the office and hit the elevator, taking it to the eighth floor and to Unit 8105. I knock on the door, the sound echoing down the hallway of white walls and light grey carpeting. Some hipster looking guy comes around the corner and sees us. With wide eyes, he immediately turns and heads back around the corner.

"Should we…?" Tracie trails off as I shake my head.

"He's probably just paranoid," I say. There's no way he would know that we are cops just by looking at us.

When the door opens, Hailey peers through the small open space between the door and the doorframe, giving us a confused look.

"Can I help you?"

"I'm Detective Carr. This is Detective Freedman. We'd like to ask you a few questions about your involvement with *The Order of the Enlightened.*"

I flash my badge and do the usual greeting. It's tiring at a point, but I want her to know that she's talking to actual cops. People pose as LAPD all the time.

Hailey's face pales. She immediately starts messing with the end of her side braid in a fidgety manner.

"I'm not a part of that anymore," she says.

"We know. We just have some questions about them," Tracie assures her. "Can we come in?"

Hailey nods and backs away from the door. She heads into her living room with a cream-colored couch, a matching lounge seat, a glass coffee table, and a large entertainment center with a flatscreen TV and some gaming consoles. Framed video game posters adorn the white walls. She sits down, curling her feet under her. She has on a light blue tank top and white lounge shorts, probably trying to enjoy a day off. I think I've ruined those plans.

"Did you see my TikTok?" she asks.

I nod as I sit on the couch.

"You said you were part of the Order for about half a year before you left."

Hailey nods again.

"Yes, I had to leave. I kept passing out at work and was on the verge of losing my role in a highly anticipated new video game."

"And they just… let you leave?" Tracie asks, pen poised over her notepad.

Hailey huffs a little.

"They weren't happy about it. They wanted me to stay and told me that I was so close to being truly enlightened. But when I pushed back, they started threatening me, telling me that I wouldn't survive out in the world again," she says in a bitter voice.

This makes me wonder if Emilia was trying to leave too. Hailey made it out alive, though.

"Did they ever try to hurt you?" I ask.

Hailey shakes her head.

"Not physically. When I left, they cut contact with me, but I started hearing terrible rumors about me around the city. They came out of nowhere, but I knew it was them. They started whispering to people that I'm a hardcore drug user and awful things like that. They tried to ruin my career!"

Tracie writes a few notes down before looking up at her.

"Do you know of any other people who managed to leave?" she asks.

Hailey thinks for a few moments before shrugging.

"Not really. Most people remain in the Order or are bullied into staying. When people get to their breaking point, they're told all of these lies about being close to enlightenment that sucks them right back in. Oh! You should talk to Kyle Crenshaw! His wife got mixed into this mess, but she disappeared and cut off all contact with her old life to live with the Prophet."

"With Elijah Nova? Do you know where?" I question her, hearing Tracie quickly write down that information.

Hailey shakes her head.

"I don't know. Kyle doesn't know either. He's a really nice guy, so maybe you can help him find his wife," she says with a hopeful look on her face.

If this guy's wife is with Elijah, I definitely want to track her down. As Tracie takes down Kyle's information, I check the time, seeing that afternoon is starting to fade into evening. After missing the cake tasting and scrambling around all day, I suppose it's time to wrap things up for now, even if I'm dying to continue.

"Can you contact Kyle and arrange a meeting for tomorrow?" I ask Tracie once we're back in the car.

Tracie looks a bit surprised by my request, but she nods and gets on it.

By the time we get back to the station, most of the other officers on the day shift have already gone home. Tracie sets up a meeting with Kyle before heading out the door to get home to her kids, leaving me at my desk. I need to grab my things and go home to spend time with Luke, but I feel rooted to the spot.

There is so much work to do. So many leads to follow. So much evidence to sift through. I already know that I won't be able to sleep much tonight, my mind is swirling around in circles.

14

Kaitlyn

In the depths of the rich neighborhood of West Hills, Kyle Crenshaw lives in a modest craftsman house with his kids. As I sit at his dining table with Tracie to my right, a glass of cold water sweating in front of me, I can tell that this is a family home with a gaping black hole in the center of it. Things are not how they're supposed to be, and that's the fault of the Order and its influential Prophet.

"Sorry, I can't talk for too long. I have to pick the kids up," Kyle says to us as he comes to the dining table, wearing an imitation vintage Ramones T-shirt and jeans. He takes a seat and rakes his fingers through his dirty blonde hair, drawing the strands back from his forehead. He seems to be all over the place, struggling to find his footing after the disappearance of his wife.

"Thank you for meeting with us," Tracie says. "We'll be quick."

I nod in agreement, tearing my eyes away from a few toys left on the ground in the living room. I don't miss that pictures of her are still displayed. Her tennis shoes are still on the rack by the door. It's like he expects her to walk back into the house at any moment.

Hopefully, she doesn't end up like Emilia.

"When did your wife disappear?" I ask him.

"A few months ago. I knew that something was up with Nicole, but I couldn't stop her from leaving," Kyle explains as he shakes his head. "I don't understand how she could just leave her own family behind like that."

I can hear the way his throat tightens and how it makes his voice sound punchy and strained. He's still reeling from it all, and I don't know if he's going to have the ending that he wants.

"Take us back to the beginning. When did things start to feel weird?" I ask.

Kyle joins his hands together in front of himself, drawing in a breath before continuing.

"Okay, so… she started doing yoga. It was

fine. Normal. She was following this one girl on Instagram, and I guess they got into contact. Nicole was invited to a yoga retreat, and she ended up going to quite a few of them."

"Did you know that it was more than a simple yoga retreat?" I ask.

Kyle shrugs.

"After a few of them went by and she started acting weird and not eating. I asked her about what she was doing, and she told me about the Order. About trying to achieve enlightenment and all that. She'd lost her mom earlier in the year, so I figured she was just trying to channel her grief into something. I should've told her to stop then," he sighs, regret glinting in his brown eyes.

"You didn't know how extreme this group was. Most people don't until it's too late," Tracie says. "And things got worse from then on?"

"Yeah, she told me she got invited to the Prophet's house in Santa Barbara. I didn't like that. Not one bit. I told her not to go, but she snapped at me, saying I was undermining her progress and making it difficult for her to rise through the levels. Whatever the hell that means."

"At this point, was she exhibiting any other

strange behavior?" I question him as I glance around once more. The house looks normal and homey.

Kyle deflates slightly.

"Everything became different. She used to take the kids to baseball and soccer practice. Never missed a single game. Once she got involved in the Order, she hardly showed up and didn't even seem to care about them. It was all about the Order and making the Prophet happy," Kyle huffs with disappointment.

It consumed her life like it did the others. Elijah must really get inside these peoples' heads to make them neglect their lives, to submit to his influence and rules.

"Did you ask her not to leave?" Tracie asks.

Kyle nods as he looks down at his hands.

"Over and over. She refused, and every single time I asked, it pushed her further away from me. After a big fight, I came home from work to see that she'd packed her stuff and disappeared. She didn't even pick up the kids that day."

"Did you file a missing person's report?"

I know I'm pushing on a sore spot, but I need as much information as I can get.

Kyle scoffs and looks up at me.

"Of course. The cops found her, and she said that she left of her own free will. There's no case there, and they wouldn't even tell me where she was." The pain is engraved in his voice.

We talk for a little bit more, but get no more useful information. Eventually, we thank him for his time and promise to stay in touch.

Kyle takes Tracie's card. Checking his watch, he sighs and pushes himself up to his feet.

"I need to go pick up my kids."

"How are they handling things?" I ask.

Kyle shakes his head.

"I don't even know what to tell them. I've said that she's on another retreat, but they're starting to not believe that. I don't know what I'm going to do," he murmurs.

I'm not the greatest at expressing sympathy. I believe that taking action works better, but I give him a small smile and a nod. He doesn't deserve this. His kids don't deserve this.

"Let's go," I tell Tracie before heading out of the house, grey clouds filling the sky up ahead and masking most of the sunlight.

Another kind of storm cloud has rolled over Hollywood ever since news about Emilia's death got out to the public. Rumors float up and down each street. Ex-boyfriend. Jealous co-star. None of it fits so far, but I'm not feeding the vultures a speck of information.

"We have to talk to this so-called Prophet," I say.

15

Emilia

One month before the SAG Awards

Sunlight washed over me as I lay back in a yellow lounge chair, watching the water in the infinity pool ripple. From here, the water seemed to blend into the shimmering deep blue of the Pacific Ocean out in the distance as the sunshine glinted off the surface. Here in the Santa Barbara hills, it felt like I had stepped into something out of a dream - so different from all the mayhem of my life in LA.

Elijah's two-story home with soaring ceilings, intricate woodwork, and luxurious furnishings was heaven. He took luxury living to the next level, and between the view and the lush, immaculately tended greenery, this place felt like the garden of Eden. And I was one of the few who had access to it.

I stretched my legs out in front of me, admiring the tan that I was starting to develop. I could take a dip, but I would have to get ready for a ritual soon, and I knew I couldn't be late. The rules were firm in the Order, but we all needed structure to keep our priorities straight.

I was lucky to be in the Order, to let them help me escape from the disastrous party scene. Hollywood was the place of my dreams, but it was also a black hole that sucked away people's motivation and happiness. It was hard being an actress and living in the public eye.

Coming here was an escape. Part of me almost didn't want to return to the city, not when I felt like I was in heaven.

An electric buzzing stole me from my thoughts, prompting me to look over at my phone on the white, metal side table next to my lounge chair. My screen lit up with a phone call. A name flashed: '*Connor Kapowski*'. A shudder of unease threatened to pass through me as I turned away from my phone, letting the call go to voicemail.

I wasn't talking to him.

But when my phone dinged to let me know that a voicemail had been left, I couldn't push away my curiosity. With a sigh, no longer feeling relaxed, I brought it to my ear.

"Hey, Sarah. I know it's been a while, but I'm coming to L.A. for a business trip. It'd be nice to see you and catch up. I know you're busy, but just let me know. Bye."

My jaw clenched, crossing my arms as I sank back into my chair. I couldn't believe he had the nerve to ask me to hang out with him. Then again, he had the nerve to do a lot of things.

"Thought I'd find you out here!"

I turned and saw my friend, Madison Bishop, walking toward me, her wavy, brown hair seeming to bounce against her back with each step. She had a long, slender figure, accented by her light blue bikini. At twenty-five, she had already made a name for herself as an assistant director of a crime television show. A USC film school grad and a known hard worker in the industry, she certainly had some aspects about her that made me a bit jealous.

Then again, she was born in Santa Barbara, while I was born in the middle of a cornfield.

Her parents still worked in the industry and advised her on the right internships to pursue. It was easier to jump in early when she was so close to everything already. I had to work hard to get out here and simply afford a roof over my head.

Still, though, despite her advantages Madison was a hustler. She never took anything for granted and always put in the extra hours. I guess that was one of the reasons why we were friends.

We were both go-getters. That was why we also took the initiative to change our lives for the better and join the Order.

"Connor called me," I said in a bitter voice as she sat down in the chair next to mine. I didn't want to be pessimistic because that put a dark cloud over everything, but Connor was a sore spot for me.

Madison's recently tinted eyebrows lifted in surprise.

"Did you pick up?" she asked before taking my bottle of tanning lotion off the table and spreading some down her long legs.

"No! I don't ever want to talk to him again," I sat up, feeling too wound up to relax. I came out here for peace and to escape the chaos in the city. Elijah taught us to get in touch with ourselves and seek enlightenment in everything that we do. It's an inspiring message, but it is definitely easier said than done. "He left me a voicemail."

"Really? What did he say?" Madison asked.

I let her listen before I deleted it. Just hearing his voice made my stomach churn, and the fact that he would be in the same city as me, made me want to hop on a flight to Europe to get as far away from him as I could.

Madison's eyes gradually widened as she listened.

"Wow, are you going to meet up with him?"

"I didn't even want to answer the phone," I reminded her with a pointed look. "He doesn't get to just drop into my life with a single call. One of the reasons why I wanted to move all the way out here was to get *away* from him!"

Madison nodded with a sympathetic look on her face.

"He really hurt you," she murmured.

I lowered my eyes and shook my head. That wasn't even the half of it.

"He wouldn't leave me alone. You know, I was scared that he would somehow follow me to California," I said, full on ranting, unable to stop the words from flowing. "Now, he's actually coming here and wants to see me. I can't get rid of him!"

Madison got up and sat beside me, putting her arm around me to pull me closer.

"I know. I know," she murmured in a comforting voice as she hugged me against her side. "You don't have to see him. He doesn't even know that you're not in LA right now. It'll be ten times harder for him to find you here."

I breathed in deeply through my nose and nodded, figuring she was right. Maybe Elijah would let me stay here while Connor was in town, but I didn't want to push things. The last thing I wanted to do was upset the Prophet after all he had done for me.

"Yeah, that's true. I'll just keep busy," I said, knowing that I would continue to overthink.

Madison gave me a squeeze.

"Hey! How about we do something fun? We can go hiking or there's that sushi place that looks really cool that we can try out."

She was the outdoorsy and try-it-all type, always seeking some sort of adventure, whether it was big or small. Anything was better than thinking about Connor.

"Sure, that sounds great," I said with a

grateful smile. She always came through for me, and I was glad that we took the dive into the Order together.

"Great!" Madison quipped before returning to her chair to lay out and tan.

I laid back down and breathed in deeply, trying to relax. I wasn't going to see him again. He would come to Los Angeles and go home. At least, that was what I hoped would happen.

If our paths crossed again, things might only get worse for me than they were before.

16

Kaitlyn

The bold smell of coffee fills the busy café where Tracie and I sit occupying a small table in the back corner. We've got a few leads under our belt and have spoken to some interesting people, yet plenty of things still aren't clear. This may be one of the most complicated cases I've ever been put on.

Adrenaline courses through me as I sip on my cappuccino and the mixture of excitement and caffeine will help me get through this new day.

I had just talked to Emilia's mom on the phone and she was inconsolable. She deserves to know what happened to her daughter.

"I think we should search for more people to

talk to," Tracie tells me before cutting into her scone.

I lift an eyebrow as I watch her eat. Who eats a scone with a fork and a knife?

"Already ahead of you," I show her my phone screen.

Tracie leans closer to take a better look.

"Madison Bishop?"

I nod and pull my phone away to look down at Madison's Instagram feed.

"She tagged Emilia in a bunch of pictures, so they must be friends. We should talk to her and see if she knows anything."

"Let's start there," Tracie agrees and continues to chew.

My knee bounces under the table as I down the rest of my cappuccino. Once Tracie finishes, we head out to my car.

"Where are we going?" she asks, ready to type an address into the GPS.

I crack a smile. Now, she's starting to get me. We grated on each other at first, but we're starting to figure out how each other operates.

"Madison's work. She's an assistant director for *Night Crime*. She posts about being on set, so it wasn't hard to figure out where it's at. I made a few calls," I say before showing her the address to put in.

"Everything is online nowadays. It's dangerous," Tracie sighs as she types in the address.

"Do you let your kids have social media?" I ask.

"They're teenagers. It's hard to keep them off the Internet, but I trust them," Tracie says before glancing over. "Do you have kids?"

I shake my head as I pull away from the café, heading to Burbank where the sound stages are located.

"No. Luke and I are just engaged."

"Oh, congrats."

I glance over at her and give her a faint smile.

"Thanks. So, I want to find out what she knows about Emilia, I also want to see if she knows anything about the Order, but we need to be circumspect. If she is involved and we go at the Order directly, she might shut down."

"Yeah, of course," Tracie says, pausing for a moment. "So, have you guys decided on a date for the wedding?"

I'm caught off-guard by the question. I thought we were talking about the case.

"Oh… um, in about a month or so I think."

The date has already slipped my mind, but I've just been so busy on this case.

"That's great. I bet it'll be one of the best days of your life."

I give her a smile. I don't say anything for the rest of the drive, and she doesn't ask me any other questions. It's not that I don't like talking about getting married. I'm just so hyper-focused on the task at hand. It's hard to tear my mind away from it.

"That's a lot of people," Tracie murmurs as we drive past the security guard, who asks for our identification, and into the parking lot near the sound stage that Madison tagged in one of her posts.

A swarm of cast members, crew, and extras filter in and out, some are lingering outside for a break.

I park and get out of my car, easily blending in with all the other people. No one questions us as we head onto the sound stage, which essentially looks like a huge warehouse on the outside. Inside, there are even more people and a bunch of constructed sets with some green screen walls in the back. One set looks like the interior of a police department while another set looks like a street corner. Hollywood magic, right?

"Slim brunette," I remind Tracie.

"That's a bit vague," she says, gesturing to a number women who meet my description a few feet away from us.

I head toward the area where there are cameras set up, hearing someone giving directions to two actors on one of the office sets. Sure enough, I see the back of a brunette's head as she sits in a director's chair next to the guy barking orders. Unfortunately, I'm about to mess up their schedule a little.

"Madison Bishop?" I say as we approach.

Madison turns and gives us a perplexed look.

"That's me," she replies as she gets off her chair to meet us halfway. She wears a stylish pair of black linen pants and a fitted, beige tank top. Once we show her our badges, her confused expression deepens. "Is everything okay?"

"We need to talk to you about Emilia Cruz. Do you have a minute?"

I say that in the form of a question, but I hope she knows that I'm not actually asking but telling.

Madison's eyes widen.

"Oh... yes," she holds her finger up to the director to let him know that she'll be gone for a moment, prompting him to announce a lunch break for everyone.

She leads us off of the sound stage to a small trailer where we have privacy. She takes a seat on the couch and folds her hands together in her lap. "When I heard about her... passing... I couldn't believe it."

She hesitates, choosing the word carefully, and definitely not the one that I would have gone with. Emilia didn't exactly die in her sleep after a short illness.

Tracie sits on the other side of the couch, and I take a seat on the small lounge seat across from Madison.

"Can you tell me about your relationship with Emilia?" I ask her.

Madison glances between us and nods.

"Yeah, we've been friends for a few years. We met at a bar and got to talking. Found out we were both in the film and television industry, so we had some things in common," she smiles. "She was one of the sweetest people I ever knew, and so talented too."

Tracie nods.

"Do you know if she had any enemies?"

Madison shakes her head.

"Enemies? No. At least she didn't tell me about any. So many people loved her. Yeah, there were haters on the Internet, but everyone has those. I can't think of anyone who would actually do this to her."

"And the two of you were in the Order?" I ask.

I hadn't planned on bringing it up like this, but Madison appears to be so unbothered by her good friend's brutal murder that I felt like I should do something to shake things up.

Madison isn't as fazed by my question as I had expected her to be. "Yes, I'm still involved, but we both were in it when she was alive."

"And no tension came from that? She didn't do something or break a rule that got her in trouble?" I ask, trying to push her.

Madison shakes her head and barks out a short laugh.

"No, of course not. It wasn't anything too serious like that. We just went on yoga retreats and did some positive thinking zoom meetings from time to time. It was a way to relax and find some meaning."

Tracie and I share a perplexed look. She is

making it sound like a casual Sunday afternoon book club.

"And how long have you been involved with the Order?" Tracie asks.

Madison shrugs.

"About a year. It's helped me manage my stress. As you can imagine, things are pretty fast paced around here."

Tracie pokes around a little more, but Madison is steadfast. She isn't pressured in the slightest, and she answers all the questions we have about Emilia and the Order without becoming frazzled. According to her, the Order is only a positive. Madison isn't giving me much, but maybe she doesn't have much to tell.

"And nothing upset Emilia at any point before she was murdered? Did anything make her mad or scared?" I ask, starting to feel desperate.

Madison thinks for a second and then her eyebrows dart up.

"Well, we were in Santa Barbara one day, and she freaked out because her ex-boyfriend called her and told her he was coming into town and wanted to see her."

"What's his name?" Tracie asks, jumping on the question before I can.

"Connor Kapowski. They were, like, high school sweethearts, but she broke up with him because he was being really weird," Madison replies, screwing up her face a little in dismay.

"How?" I ask.

"Like stalking her. He wouldn't ever leave her alone. Los Angeles was her shot at not only chasing her dream but getting away from *him*. She was really upset by his call."

"Thank you, we'll look into that," Tracie rises to her feet.

I still have one more question.

"What were you two doing in Santa Barbara?"

"Oh, just visiting a friend," Madison says casually before looking between us with a cheeky smile. Somebody calls her name, and she has to go. "If you have any more questions, you know where to find me."

Tracie looks at me, and I shake my head. We've got what we need for now.

"I want to find this Connor guy," I say, following Tracie to my car.

"We need to write our reports," she points out. "We have to get all of these interviews on paper."

I grimace. One of the worst parts of my job

is doing the paperwork, but we may as well get our reports done and our information organized before we do more interviews. I check the time and sigh, seeing that it's already almost noon.

"Alright, let's be quick about it," I say before heading to the station, dreading the rest of the afternoon.

17

Kaitlyn

My eyelids start to grow heavy as my fingers clunkily move over my keyboard, typing out my report on our interview with Richard Murphy. Based on the slow typing from Tracie's desk, she's going even slower than I am.

Usually I enjoy doing the reports but this time I can't wait to get back into the field. Plus, I'm dying for another cappuccino. We've done quite a few interviews, and I know that it's going to take me forever. Looking at the digital clock on the bottom right of my computer screen, I withhold a groan. I'm not going to finish today.

I save what I have of my report and stand from my seat, hastily gathering my things. I don't want to leave the station, but if I don't leave right now, Luke is going to be mad. I promised him that we'd do this today, and honestly, I just want to go ahead and get it over with.

"I have to go. I'll be back later," I say. I'm definitely coming back afterward to get some more work done, even if it's only for an hour or two. Time is of the essence with this case. With *any* case.

Tracie looks up with a confused look.

"Where are you going?"

I shrug.

"I just… have an appointment."

"Are you feeling okay?"

I can't get anything past her. If I say one lie, it's going to roll into another, and she'll find a loose string somewhere.

"I have to try on wedding dresses at a boutique."

"You're picking out your wedding dress *today*?" Tracie gasps.

I nod. I have to make the decision today, but I don't even know what kind of dress suits me.

"Who's going with you to help? Your mom? Maid of honor?" Tracie asks as she rests her chin on the top of her hand.

I shake my head, feeling a bit embarrassed about my answer. Most people have at least one person with them when looking for a wedding dress.

"No one. Just me."

Tracie's eyes grow wide.

"What? No, you need someone there with you to give you a second opinion. Why don't I come along and help?"

A jolt of surprise hits me. We hardly even know each other.

"You want to? Don't you have work to do?"

Tracie waves her hand dismissively as she gets to her feet and grabs her bag.

"I can finish it later. Shopping for your wedding dress is a memory you'll have forever. What boutique are we going to?"

"Hollander," I say letting her take the lead.

I won't admit it aloud but having her with me makes me feel a little less nervous about picking out a dress. I can't have Luke with me, I don't want to invite my mom, and Violet is so far away. My old friend Sydney is on a trip. It's just me, but I'm glad Tracie will be there to at least give me a second opinion. Fashion isn't my thing, but I don't want to look bad on my wedding day.

"I've heard good things about that place,"

Tracie says as she gets into the passenger's seat of my car.

I get in and look over at her.

"So, you've been through it all? Wedding and all that?"

Tracie nods.

"I was married for almost fourteen years before my husband passed away."

My face nearly drops. I didn't expect the conversation to shift in that direction.

"I'm sorry," I say. I can't count how many times I've told someone that I'm sorry for their loss. I probably give my condolences more than congratulate people. "How did he pass?"

"Cancer. Pancreatic," Tracie says, a gentle sigh breaking from her. "But those years I got to spend with him were some of the best of my life. I'll never forget the day I picked out *my* dress."

My mind shifts to Luke, thinking about how lost I'd feel without him.

"I'm sure it was beautiful," I say as I pull away from the station.

Tracie smiles.

"We were just kids and it was. Do you have any ideas for what kind of dress you might want?"

I know that I should be more prepared. I should have a Pinterest board full of ideas but I don't. I haven't even really thought about it much.

"Not really," I admit. "I don't wear dresses all that often, so I don't have much to go off of."

Tracie nods, but looks scandalized.

"That's okay. We'll figure it out and find the perfect one," she assures me. "Some people have a vision of their perfect day for years and some do it more on the fly. My flower arrangement was last minute because I just couldn't decide between the roses or the anemones."

Her words actually make me feel a little better. I still have a little time to get my affairs in order, but I know that Luke is getting antsy as the day approaches. He's better at this type of stuff than I am.

"What did you pick?" I ask. I don't even know what anemones are.

"White roses," Tracie smiles. Her eyes seem distant like she's deep in thought.

I stay silent, letting my stomach turn as my anxiety starts to build. Thoughts race through my head, and I can't help but feel overwhelmed. I want this day to be perfect, but I also want to be comfortable and confident in my own skin.

I don't know what kind of dress is flattering on my figure or if I'll be able to navigate a long train. One thing is for sure, I don't want to look like some fairytale princess.

I want to look like me, and who knows if I can even achieve that in something as extravagant and bold as a wedding dress.

18

Kaitlyn

As I step into the upscale wedding boutique in Culver City, I am immediately enveloped in an atmosphere of elegance and luxury. The interior is decorated with tasteful chandeliers, plush velvet seating, and shimmering gold accents, giving the boutique a regal feel. The walls are adorned with photographs of glamorous brides in their designer gowns, and the racks of dresses are arranged in a neat and organized fashion. Every dress is a work of art, with intricate details, delicate lace, and shimmering beads.

I knew that the boutique would have a lot of options, but I didn't expect there to be *hundreds* of dresses to choose from. As I peruse, I can't help but feel awed by the exquisite craftsmanship and attention to detail. Each dress seems more beautiful than the last, and I start to feel like a princess trying on her ball gown, which makes me somewhat uncomfortable.

"Oh, boy," I suck in some breath, trying to stay centered. I don't even know where to start.

"Hi! You must be Kaitlyn. I'm Stella. I'll be helping you today," a cheery redhead greets me. She's about my age, impeccably dressed in a chic black dress.

"Hi," I say, tensing up slightly as her eyes roam over me, mentally taking my measurements. At a crime scene, I know exactly what to do. But here, I'm lost.

"I'm Tracie. We work together," Tracie introduces herself.

"Awesome! How about we talk styles? What are you thinking?" Stella asks the questions that I don't have any answers to.

I glance at Tracie in a silent plea for help.

"Nothing too flashy. Something between modest and bold to really bring out her best features," Tracie speaks for me.

Stella thinks for a second before a smile pops up on her face.

"Let me show you a few dresses. You can let

me know what you think about the cuts and then we'll get you some that you want to try on," she leads us to the back. There's a sitting area in front of a small, raised platform for me to stand on, a mirror, and a changing room.

I squint slightly as I sit down on the cream-colored sofa, waiting for Stella to pick out a few selections, my knee automatically starts bouncing.

"This definitely isn't your scene, huh?" Tracie asks nudging me.

I smirk a little.

"Not really," I shrug. "I love Luke, but all of this wedding stuff…"

"It's a lot, but you'll look back on your wedding day and even appreciate moments like these," Tracie tries to reassure me.

We'll see.

"Here we go! I've picked out three options to get a better idea of what style you're looking for," Stella comes over, pulling a rack on wheels behind her. She presents the first dress. "This is a satin, off-the-shoulder classic gown. Simple but elegant and modern with a chapel train."

I wrinkle my nose a little before I can control my expression. In theory, it's a pretty dress, but it just doesn't strike me as something I want to even try on.

"It's a bit too… plain. I mean, I don't want anything too glamorous, but…" I trail off, not even knowing what I want.

"No, I agree. It's a bit lacking," Tracie backs me up.

"Here is the second option," Stella directs our attention to the next dress. "This is our strapless, lace mermaid dress. It has a chapel train as well and a plunging sweetheart neckline."

"I don't want it to be so tight. The lace is nice, but I don't think I want my shoulders so exposed. I get cold pretty easily."

Stella's eyebrows pop up.

"Oh! Well, I think this next dress might suit you better," she says, pulling out the third dress, which catches my eye. "This is our satin dress with an A-line skirt and a lace-appliqued bodice. As you see, there's lace, long sleeves and a sweep train."

I find myself getting to my feet and walking closer to the dress and inspecting it. It's pretty fancy, but it's not overwhelming. The chest portion is covered with intricate lace, and the sweep train isn't as long as the chapel train. It's much subtler.

"I think I like this one."

"You should try it on. See how it looks," Tracie encourages me. When my expression wavers a little, she gives me a pointed look to ground me. "Trying it on doesn't mean you're committing to it. Just give it a chance."

I nod and turn to Stella.

"Ok, let's do it."

"Great! I'll adjust the size as we go."

Not knowing what that means, I change out of my work clothes and pull on the dress most of the way up, letting Stella zip it up and attach big clams to the back to tailor the dress around my body. She adjusts the plunging neckline and sleeves before leading me out to the platform.

I don't even make it fully out of the dressing room before I hear Tracie gasp.

"You look beautiful!"

The bridal suite is spacious and luxurious, with plush seating, and a full-length mirror. The lighting is perfect, allowing me to see every intricate detail, from the delicate lace to the sparkling beading.

I smirk and shake my head, feeling my face burn as I step onto the platform. In the mirror, I see my flushed face however, my eyes trail down to take in my dress and how it hugs my figure. The plunging neckline exposes my neck and collarbones, but the sleeves cover my shoulders and arms. That levels things out.

"It's nice," I say as I smooth my hands down my sides. It certainly brings out my curves.

"Nice? It's amazing!" Tracie assures me as she and Stella share a smile.

I take another look, the corner of my mouth turning up slightly. I do a turn, examining my sides and back and how the train seems to float around me. I didn't think that something would catch my eye this fast.

"Can I FaceTime my sister and see what she thinks?" I ask.

Stella nods and walks off.

"You have a sister?" Tracie asks.

I nod as I find Violet's contact in my phone.

"She's fifteen and living back at home with our mom in Big Bear Lake," I press the call button. It only rings for a few seconds before Violet picks up.

"Hey, what's up?" Violet greets me, holding the camera above her as she lays in bed. Her long hair is splayed out on the pillow and her eyes are lined in heavy raccoon eyeliner, just the way she likes it. Her red lips make her skin look even more pale.

"Hey, I'm trying on wedding dresses and may have found one I like. Do you want to see it and let me know what you think?"

Violet sits up, smiling ear to ear.

"Of course!"

I turn a little so that Violet can see Tracie behind me.

"This is Tracie. She's my partner."

I hand her my phone so that she can switch the camera and show a full-length view of me in my dress. Having a camera on me automatically makes me want to look away, but I steel myself and fluff out my train a little so that Violet can see all of the details of the dress.

"It's beautiful, Kait! You have to get it! Luke will love it!" Violet gushes.

"You think so?" I ask. I do like the dress, and if Violet and Tracie like it too, I'm sure Luke will as well. I can see myself walking down the aisle in this and still feeling comfortable. That's the most important thing.

"I'm so excited! It's about time you two got married!"

"I know. I know."

She adores Luke and has been pushing me

to hurry up and get married to him. He's an amazing guy, and I know that he'll be a great husband.

"Tell me you're getting this dress."

I take the phone from Tracie and flip the camera so that it faces me.

"I'll get the dress," I promise, smiling as she throws her free hand up in victory. It's really great seeing her happy again. After the kidnapping, I thought that she would carry the trauma with her for a very long time, but it seems like her mood is improving a lot. Therapy is helping for sure. I just hope she continues to get better.

I want to stay on the phone longer, but Violet pushes me to buy the dress and for us to catch up at another time. Once we hang up, I look for Stella.

"She's helping someone else."

While I wait, I decide to do a little casual digging. The next person I want to talk to is Connor Kapowski, and it's too easy to find his Twitter. And the fact that he just tweeted a few minutes ago.

"Look!" I say as I stride over to Tracie, flashing her my phone.

She leans closer to look at the picture of

Connor and two other guys seated at a restaurant.

"What is it?" she asks, not knowing what she's looking at.

"That's Connor," I tell her as I point at the guy with sandy blonde hair that's purposely styled as slightly unruly and tousled, that beach or athletic look. "He just made a post about being at Carlito's on Melrose!"

"But we're not finished," Tracie says as she gestures to my dress.

Connor may be posting after leaving the restaurant, but if there's a chance that he's there and we can catch him by surprise, I'm jumping on that. I search the place until I find Stella.

"I want the dress," I tell her, stealing her attention away from some other young, pink-cheeked bride.

"Wonderful! Would you like any modifications?"

I shake my head.

"I just want it how it is, but I can't take it right now. I'll come back for it. Here's my card. I'm getting changed," I say as I put my credit card in her hand before dashing to the changing room. I grab Tracie's arm and tug her into the room with me. "Unzip me. We need to move fast."

Tracie doesn't protest and helps me get out of the dress. She puts it back on the rack and waits outside the changing room.

I'm out in under a minute, picking up my card and receipt at the front desk and flying out the door.

19

Kaitlyn

After making the drive to West Hollywood and struggling to find a parking spot around Melrose Avenue, I lead Tracie to Carlito's Gardel, an upscale Argentine restaurant. I walk inside and peer around the dining area, which is full of white-clothed tables, string lights, and sleek wooden chairs. It's bustling with people, and I try to take a look at every single person to see if Connor is still here.

"Hi, how many?" the hostess asks.

"We're still waiting on some people. We're not sure who's going to make it yet," Tracie says to get her to back off.

I look to the left toward the back, narrowing my eyes slightly as I focus in on a man wearing the same short-sleeve, white button-down that Connor was wearing in the picture. Sure enough, I see the blonde hair too.

"There he is," I say, pointing him out as he sits in the back with two friends around his age.

"I thought he was from Iowa."

"Must be here for business again. Or something else," I say before leading her out of the restaurant. "We'll catch him when he leaves. I want him to be alone."

Tracie nods in agreement, and we linger by the full parking lot, waiting for Connor to get finished with his steak and whiskey or whatever guys like him drink. It takes him almost an hour to part ways with his buddies and walk toward his car.

"Mr. Kapowski. Do you have a minute?" I call out as we approach.

Connor whips around and tilts his head slightly.

"Hello," he greets us. "Who are you?"

Once I get closer, I realize how tall he is. He used to be an all-star baseball player and his broad shoulders and muscular arms show that he still has the physique. The bright blue eyes make him a shoo-in for a small-town heartthrob.

"I'm Detective Carr. This is Detective Freeman. We'd like to ask you a few questions."

"Okay, no problem," Connor relaxes, crossing his arms over his chest in a casual manner.

"What are you doing here?" I ask. He's not from around this area, so it's interesting to me that he's here around the same time his ex-girlfriend was murdered.

"I'm here for business. I was just meeting with some executives from Sprout. It's a plant-based company. They're wanting to work with my soybean farm," he explains with a small smile. "I don't know why they want to work with little ol' me out in Iowa, but I'm stoked."

Finding him a bit hard to read, I pause.

"Are you aware of Emilia Cruz's death?" Tracie asks.

Connor frowns and nods as he glances down at the ground.

"Yeah, I heard about Sarah. I actually haven't talked to her in a few months, but we used to be really close before she moved out here. It was terrible hearing about her death. I saw her mom not too long ago… it's awful."

"Why did you reach out to her a few months

ago?" I ask, searching his face for a hint of a confession.

Connor shrugs.

"I was going to be in town for business, and I wanted to reconnect with an old friend. We've known each other since we were kids and she's the only person I know around here."

"That's interesting," I cross my arms.

Connor cocks an eyebrow at me.

"What's that?"

"Well, we spoke to a friend of Emilia's, and she said that you weren't asking to see her as an old friend but as an ex-boyfriend who wouldn't leave her alone."

I watch his reaction.

"What? Who said that?" he asks in a state of shock.

"We can't disclose that information," Tracie says as she holds her hand up to signal for him to take a breath.

Shaking his head, Conner draws in a deep breath, exhaling quickly.

"I didn't stalk her. Ever. I only called her that one time, and she never called me back. I took that as a hint and didn't reach out to her again."

My jaw tenses as he stands his ground. Why

would Emilia lie to Madison if she broke up with him? There are too many missing pieces and I have no idea what to believe.

Just as I'm about to say something else, Conner glances at his phone.

"I'm sorry. I have another meeting starting soon. I can give you my number if you want to ask any other questions, though."

Tracie nods and takes down his information.

I know that coincidences happen, but the timing of her death and him being in town is certainly interesting. Even if he didn't actually murder her, I can't help but wonder if he still had any part to play in what happened.

"Come on. Let's go back to the station," Tracie says and I let her lead me back even though that's the last place I want to be. I don't want to sit around. I want to talk to more people. I want to find another lead.

"We can check Emilia's phone records to confirm his statement. Did he actually only call her once?" Tracie asks.

Now, that's a good idea.

20

Kaitlyn

"Alright, here we go," I say as I scroll through Emilia's phone records once we log into her mobile phone account. This is easier than getting a search warrant and waiting for the phone company, and it's perfectly legal since she is dead, and we have her laptop.

"I need to get glasses," she mutters, moving her chair closer.

I smirk slightly and scroll through the records to a few months ago, seeing plenty of calls between Emilia and Madison and Emilia and Richard. She stays in constant contact with her mom and other cast members as well. It's hard to wade through all the calls, but I eventually see an Iowa number listed under Connor's name.

"Here's the first call," I tell Tracie, who jots the time down. "She didn't pick up, so he left a voicemail."

Tracie nods, motioning for me to continue.

I scroll down a little bit, and then a bit further. Besides her mom's number, there isn't another call from Iowa whatsoever.

"Well, damn. He didn't call her again," I mutter sitting back in my chair.

"There are other ways to be reached. Text messages. Emails. Social media," Tracie points out.

I crack my knuckles and sit back up, reaching over to grab the notepad with Emilia's passwords written down. We were lucky to find a document on her laptop where she jotted down all her passwords so that she didn't forget them. I doubt she ever expected the police to use them to solve her murder.

"Let's check them all," I say.

The process takes hours. Having to log into her accounts and then meticulously search for any messages from Connor is incredibly time-consuming, but we're thorough, not wanting to miss a thing. Eventually, we reach the conclusion that Conner has not had any correspondence with Emilia, at least not as far as we can see.

"I don't get it," I mutter in annoyance as I finish checking Emilia's Instagram DMs.

"She may have other accounts that she didn't put down," Tracie points out. "Evidently, celebrities use fake accounts all the time."

I nod considering the possibility. Emilia may have a secret account, but I don't know how to find it. She wasn't logged into any on her phone or her laptop, so I don't even know where to begin to look for it.

"Well, that's a bust for now," I sigh.

Tracie taps her pen against her notepad, her eyebrows knitting together in thought.

"I still think we should keep an eye on him. Just in case," she says, speaking my mind.

"Absolutely. I don't trust him."

"I better get home and start on dinner for the kids. Are you done for the day?" she asks, getting up.

I need to do something before I go home. I won't be able to sleep or relax unless I have a game plan for tomorrow.

"Not yet. I'm going to order Chinese and work on the reports," I say, hoping that I can find some sort of clue as I write those out. Maybe I missed some tiny detail that may bring me to an important lead.

"Don't work too hard," Tracie says, patting my shoulder. "You looked stunning in your dress."

My face heats up and I give her a coy smile, thanking her for coming with me.

"Goodnight," I say, watching her head out of the station.

Turning back to the computer, I put in my usual order of lo mien and crab Rangoon at the local Chinese place a few streets over and get back to work.

As I wait for my food to arrive, it dawns on me that Emilia's life was far more complicated than she wanted to let on. I have no idea where all of these strands will lead me, but I know that her murderer is out there and he can't hide forever.

Once my Chinese is delivered, I put my work on the back burner as I swirl my fork around in my bowl of noodles. I hadn't eaten anything besides breakfast today, so I'm starving. I reach for my phone to send Luke a text to let him know that I'll be late again, but my phone rings with an incoming call.

"Is this Detective Carr? This is Kyle Crenshaw. We talked the other day," a shaky voice speaks.

I immediately sit up straight, dropping my fork in the bowl.

"Yes, what's going on?" I ask, listening to his labored breathing.

"I… uh… oh my God…" he starts to sob. "It's Nicole."

My heart races as I try to make out his words. He gets so choked up that I can hardly understand anything that he's saying.

"What about Nicole? Kyle, talk to me."

"She… they found her… she's dead," Kyle cries, stumbling over his words.

My eyes widen. Nicole Crenshaw, a known follower of the Prophet, the woman who ditched her family to live with him is dead.

"Where? Where did they find her?" I ask, abandoning my dinner and my report.

"Five Star Motel… in Ventura," Kyle mumbles.

I write down the name on a sticky note before ripping it off the pad.

"The police are saying it's a suicide. But it's not! She'd never commit suicide! This is the Order!" Kyle yells, his grief morphing into anger.

I get in my car and put the address into my GPS.

"I'm heading over there now. I'll get to the bottom of this."

"Please, Detective… please tell them the Order did this. She wouldn't have done this to herself. Oh… Nicole…"

21

Kaitlyn

It's about an hour and a half to get to Ventura from Los Angeles, but it takes me about twenty minutes less as I swerve through traffic, driving thirty miles over the speed limit.

What was Nicole doing in that dock town anyway? Working class Ventura was a far cry from upscale Santa Barbara. I can't think of any reason for Nicole to be there, but I hope that the crime scene offers some clues. When I approach the motel, I realize that yet another member of the Order has been found dead.

A gas station, an old fast-food place, and a liquor store line the street. It doesn't take me long to see the faded yellow sign with red letters, which reads 'Five Star Motel.' As expected, there are flashing police lights in the parking lot and caution tape blocking off one of the rooms. I park next to an ambulance and watch the paramedics head in with a gurney and a body bag.

A few police officers linger outside talking to each other. I pull out my badge and walk up to them.

"Detective Carr. What's going on?"

"Officer Martinez," one of the older cops introduces himself. "Looks like an overdose."

"Really? Why do you say that?"

"I know a druggie hideout when I see one," one of the other cops says. "White powder on the floor. Empty baggies. Vomit on her face. She's dirty and pale. We'll have to do a toxicology exam, but you must know what this looks like."

Without saying a word, I peer into the room watching them process the scene. They're definitely not wrong about what it looks like. Accidental overdoses happen all the time now. With the prevalence of fentanyl and the fact that it's slipped into practically anything to increase potency, Nicole could be one of thousands of tragic cases, which are happening all over the United States.

But something still feels off.

"Are there any traces of blood in the room? Signs of a break-in?" I ask, wanting to cover all the bases.

"Nothing from what we've seen. We've scoured the room for any signs of violence. No broken glass. No broken lock on the door. No blood or torn out hair," Officer Martinez says with a shrug. "Just her body and what looks like drugs."

I chew on the inside of my cheek for a moment, trying to approach this from another angle.

"How did you know she was in here?" I ask Officer Martinez.

"Motel owner called. She hadn't paid for the last two nights, so he came over to check on her. He opened the door and found her on the floor. I don't think there's anything more to this than that, Detective. We get these calls a lot."

"He's wrong!" A loud voice stares me.

I turn around to see Kyle pushing his way past a police officer to get to me. His eyes are red and full of anguish.

"They won't listen to me! She wouldn't kill herself. She never used drugs!" Kyle shouts, a big vein the middle of his forehead throbbing with anger.

"If you do not calm down, we will detain you, sir!" one of the other cops says firmly.

"Woah, it's fine. Let me talk to him," I tell the officers before turning to Kyle. "They're saying they see drugs in the room. Are you sure she never partook of anything? Even pills?"

"What? No! She took herbal supplements and vitamins. That's it," Kyle says. "She was all about her health. She'd never put that stuff in her body!"

"Okay, okay," I say, putting my hands up to get him to calm down. "The medical examiner is going to take a look at her. She'll be able to figure out the cause of death."

"The Order did it. They killed her!" Kyle screams, the rage in his voice palpable as he slams a fist into the wall and tears stream down his cheeks. "I know it!"

My mind whirls with fury, believing the Order might have something to do with this too. Still, I force myself to keep my emotions under control.

"I'm sorry, Kyle," I say with a tinge of sadness. He hoped that she would come back to him and their kids, but instead, she found herself twisted up in a web of destruction that ended up costing her life.

Kyle lowers his head and wipes his eyes, attempting to quell his tears.

"It's not right. It's not fair," he says as we watch the medical staff wheel out his wife's body in a body bag a few minutes later.

I part my lips to try to offer him some comfort, but another voice sounds from behind me. It chills me to the bone.

"Maybe you didn't know your wife as well as you thought."

I whip around and feel my stomach drop at the sight of none other than Elijah Nova, the Prophet.

He's been on my mind for days, and here he is - standing before us with an air of arrogance.

But before I can even react, Kyle lunges at Elijah and takes him to the ground, covering him with punches.

22

Kaitlyn

It takes the officers a few moments to loop their arms around Kyle and finally pull him away from Elijah. Nevertheless, he continues to spit obscenities and threats, struggling to break free. Two officers have to dig their feet into the ground to drag him away, and I'm honestly surprised that they don't pull their guns on him.

"Mr. Nova," I say, finally snapping into action. "I need to have a word with you."

I step forward, my hand resting lightly on my gun belt as I prepare to break into a sprint if Kyle decides to run.

Elijah, on the other hand, doesn't seem to be the least bit concerned, remaining calm and collected. He merely dusts his white linen pants off and meticulously pinches and pulls at the sleeves of his olive green shirt until it's back in its right place.

"Of course. And you are?" Elijah asks as he holds his hand out to me with a mild but friendly smile. When his blue eyes settle on mine, they're so steady and unmoving that I find them unnerving.

"Detective Carr," I say, starting to reach for his hand when I suddenly catch sight of three women approaching Elijah from behind. I pause and eye them, watching them slink their way over and surround him like a shield.

"A pleasure, Detective. Though, I wish we were meeting under different circumstances," Elijah says as he gives the women, who all look to be in their early twenties and are noticeably thin, a comforting look.

An uncomfortable sensation twists in my stomach. It's clear that these women worship this man, and I wonder if Nicole felt the same way. So, what could have happened? And what about Emilia?

"Did you know Nicole well?"

Elijah gives me a non-committal gesture.

"She was a part of our wellness group, but she'd stopped coming to our meetings not too long ago. We figured she'd given up on us. The path to enlightenment is not a straightforward nor easy journey. Many give up along the way. I merely try to act as a guiding light. Unfortunately, some people lose sight of that light and venture into darkness."

I have to keep myself from narrowing my eyes. It sounds like a joke, except for the fact that he is utterly serious.

"And you didn't hear anything from her?" I ask crossing my arms over my chest.

Elijah shakes his head.

"I'm afraid not. I thought she went back to her family," he says looking over at Kyle, who is seated on the ground next to one of the police cruisers in handcuffs. "She did love them, but to best serve the people you love, you need to be the best version of yourself. She had been willing to make that sacrifice and return home a better person. I hate that she never made it to her husband and their children."

His voice sounds heavy like he feels true grief, but at the same time, it feels like an act.

"Why are you here, exactly? This is quite far from your stomping grounds," I say as I lift an eyebrow, noting how the women tighten their grip on him in a protective manner.

"Word spreads fast. There are more of us

than people think. When I heard that Nicole was finally found, I had to come see for myself," Elijah says, keeping his eyes steady on me. Has this guy even blinked yet?

"Well, this is the second member of your group to die in the last few days. It's a bit suspicious, don't you think?" I ask, trying to create a crack in his laid back exterior.

Elijah's eyes lower slightly.

"Oh, yes. Emilia," he murmurs. "When I heard of her passing, I meditated all morning, hoping that she would find enlightenment in her afterlife. She was such a hopeful beauty… I'm disgusted by the monster who did that to her."

"She didn't deserve it," one of the women with her brown hair twisted into a side braid announces. When Elijah quietly glanced over at her with a stern expression, she shut her mouth and lowered her eyes.

Elijah might have these women wrapped around his little finger, but that doesn't mean that he had anything to do with these deaths. I don't even know if Nicole's death is a murder.

"How involved with the Order would you say Nicole was?" I ask.

"She was quite involved for a while. She attended many meetings and retreats, and she'd started making a lot of progress. I was happy for her. Being able to watch someone's spirit transform is an experience unlike any other," Elijah says with a pleased smile. "But she didn't come by for several weeks. We didn't have any contact with her during that period of time up to her death."

"Do you know of any reason why she would leave so abruptly? Did she have a fight with someone?" I ask, poking around to find a weak spot.

Usually, when people are tired of something, they wean off little by little until they're able to disappear. She went cold turkey and, given her previous devotion, I don't believe that things just fizzled out.

"Of course not. We don't argue. We share our thoughts and work through misunderstandings and concerns together," Elijah says, shaking his head. "She hadn't brought up any concerns to me. If she had, I would've worked with her to make adjustments."

I doubt that's the case, but I don't argue.

"Thank you for answering my questions, Mr. Nova. I'm sure we'll be in contact again soon."

Whether he wants to be or not, he is a piece

of this puzzle, and I'm determined to find out where he fits in.

"Good luck on your search, Detective," Elijah replies before looking back over at Kyle, who is glaring at him intently. "I need to get back home anyway."

Watching him walk away makes my jaw clench. There's something off about him, but I can't quite pin it down. I still need more evidence, and that's going to be difficult to find.

This case is more troublesome and complex than most of the ones I've worked on, which means navigating this maze will not be easy. Right now, the end is nowhere in sight, but it's out there.

I head back over to Kyle, waving the other officers away so that I can crouch down in front of him. He's not a threat. He's just a grieving man, and I want to give him just a little bit of hope to help him get through this tragedy.

"I'm going to figure out what really happened to Nicole."

Kyle lifts his eyelids. He swallows hard and nods, his expression hardening.

I squeeze his arm, hoping he finds the strength to keep himself and his family together.

Things are only going to get tougher before they get better.

23

Kaitlyn

The sound of Tracie's rapid scribbling grates on me as I relay everything that has happened. Per usual, she's insistent on taking notes and making sure she has every detail written down.

"I can't believe I missed this," Tracie sighs, putting her pen down. "This Nova guy is no good."

I nod in agreement. He's one of the primary suspects for sure, but the problem is that there's little evidence that he had anything to do with either of their deaths.

"Maybe if we learn more about what happened to Nicole, we can get some clues about what led to Emilia's death," I say, hoping that there are some connections to be made between the two.

So far, the only thing we have is that they're both dead. But under very different circumstances. Nicole's death isn't even officially ruled a homicide and might never be. But the fact that they were both in the Order is important.

"Alright, let's start there," Tracie agrees with a determined nod.

I grab the phone and dial the Ventura County medical examiner's number, hitting the speaker button so that Tracie can hear too.

"Dr. Bardell? This is Detective Carr. I was on the scene earlier for Nicole Crenshaw. What do you have on her?" I ask as Tracie prepares her pen and notepad.

"Good morning, Detective. I don't have much. As you know the full toxicology report will take a few weeks to a few months to come back." Her voice is professional and distant. I've never worked with her before since this is a different jurisdiction so I can't exactly tell if she's blowing me off or is just busy.

I withhold a sigh, knowing that this is expected, but it's still annoying how long some processes take. I'm on a time-sensitive murder case, so if I have to work fast, I need everyone else to work fast too. Unfortunately, I don't have enough authority or influence to speed anything up.

"Alright, what *do* you have?" I ask, bouncing my knee. I need at least a few clues so that I can piece this puzzle together.

"Not much."

"Please, you must have something."

"The police told me they did find traces of fentanyl. I'm sure you saw the state of the hotel room. If I had to guess, I'd go with an overdose. But don't quote me on that."

My jaw tenses as I shake my head. It's a well-known fact that ever since the Sackler family and their company, Purdue Pharma, encouraged doctors all over America to over prescribe oxycodone with their intense marketing efforts, the United States has been in the midst of an opioid epidemic that has taken the lives of over half a million people and made millions more addicted to opioids. It also led to the Mexican cartels' manufacturing and distribution of fentanyl, a cheaper but much more deadly synthetic opioid, which is one hundred times more potent than morphine and fifty times more potent than heroin.

Thousands of accidental fentanyl overdoses have been reported all over the state and the country. Drug dealers began spiking other substances, like Xanax and heroin, with fentanyl in order to bolster their potency and make more money without customers knowing they are consuming something lethal.

"What about her body? Any signs of trauma?" I ask.

"No, no bruising or signs of trauma. It seems like she hasn't showered in a few days."

"Call me as soon as the toxicology report comes in or if you find anything else," I say as a heavy weight settles on my shoulders. Another dead end. Damn it.

"Will do."

I put the phone back on the receiver and turn to Tracie, who stares at her blank sheet of paper.

"Well, that was a bust," I mutter shaking my head. "It'll be weeks before we hear back, and so far we have no witnesses or information about what exactly happened in that room."

Tracie nods and gestures to my computer.

"I can look at her records and see if I find anything interesting," she offers.

"Go ahead. I have to make another call." I dial the number for the venue where my wedding will be held, rubbing my temple as I try to remember all that Luke told me to say.

I wish he would do this part, but he took care of the cake testing and the catering company, so I'm stuck with this.

"Hello! This is Sharon at the Malibu West Beach Club. How can I help you?" an overly cheery woman answers. When I introduce myself, she says that she's excited to hear from me and needs more details.

"Do you have a final headcount for the ceremony?"

So far, most have RSVP'd for the wedding, leaving us with just a little bit of guessing room.

"We're looking at around fifty. Give or take."

Thankfully, Luke is fine with it being a small event with only our closest friends and family members and their plus one's. A huge chaotic wedding would be too much for me.

"Wonderful! We got a call from your caterer, and they said you've decided on bacon-wrapped scallops for one of the appetizers served at the reception. Would you like that served directly to the guests at their seats, or would you like us to arrange a buffet where they can get their own portions?" she asks.

I nearly throw my hands up. I thought Luke took care of all these little details.

"I guess just put a table out," I reply. "They can have free rein."

"Great! I'll get that arranged for you. Now, let's talk cake presentation," Sharon says before diving into a bunch of options of where the cake can be displayed during the reception.

I close my eyes and knead the spot between them with my knuckle. My brain is at capacity at this point, largely as a result of the case. Having to try to cram all of this wedding stuff in there too gives me a headache.

"Is that all?" I ask her, hoping that I've answered all of her questions.

"I believe so! I'll give you a call if I need anything else," Sharon quips.

I return to my desk, pushing my phone away from me and hoping that it doesn't ring again unless someone can give me a tip about the case.

"Doing some more wedding planning?" Tracie asks, glancing over.

"Oh, yeah. Just the venue," I reply before taking a seat. "Find anything?"

Tracie shakes her head.

"Everything looks clean. No priors. Only

has one parking ticket," she tells me. "What place are you guys using?"

I'd rather talk about the case, but I'll satisfy her curiosity since she's been a good partner. Plus, I know that she'll loop right around back to the case.

"Malibu West Beach Club," I reply with a small shrug. "Luke picked it out."

Tracie's eyebrows shoot up.

"Wow, that's real fancy. I think I read about that place once in a magazine."

"It won't be too extravagant. Just friends and family."

Tracie laughs a little.

"Well, I didn't peg you as the big, fancy wedding type. So, what's the plan?"

"The reception will be in the club, but we'll be married out on the beach at sunset." Hopefully, there will be good weather that day. No dark clouds, June gloom, or wind. The possibility of rain is highly unlikely though, since it's summer in Southern California.

"Aw, that sounds so nice," she says with a warm smile. "That sounds more intimate."

She does have a point. Something about being on a private part of the beach away from others and not being on some stage or at the front of a church makes our ceremony feel a little more special. Like it's just for us.

Honestly, I wouldn't mind eloping. I've never been crazy about the whole wedding thing. Having to deal with family. Worrying about making sure our guests are happy. Planning every little detail. All I care about is being married to my best friend.

After a few moments, Tracie gives me some more background on Nicole. My mind isn't fully locked in, though. It trails to my upcoming wedding and all of the things that still need to fall into place. Everything in my life feels like a complex puzzle with so many missing pieces. I can't help but wonder if I'll ever finally put it all together.

24

Kaitlyn

Since Nicole is a dead end for now, I need to chase another lead. I can't sit still and scroll through databases and reports until I find some little tidbit of information that I'm desperate enough to chase. There are so many unanswered questions, so I pick the other person I'm suspicious of besides Elijah Nova.

"I think we need to refocus on Connor," I tell Tracie as we stand outside of the police station, leaning on either side of my car.

Tracie nods in agreement.

"He may not have told us everything."

"Or all he told us was lies," I point out. "She told Madison that he made her uncomfortable. Yet, he claims there was no bad blood between them. Someone is lying."

"The liars are the ones trying to cover up their secrets," Tracie adds as our eyes meet. "Ex-partners make up a large percentage of murders, especially with female victims."

She doesn't have to tell me this. It's common knowledge.

"I don't think anything is going to come out of us questioning him again. We need to ask other people. If others besides Madison back up Emilia's story of him being a stalker, that would make him more viable as a suspect," I say.

"We should go back to her apartment building and talk to the neighbors," Tracie suggests. "It's always best to look closer to home first."

She has a good point. Neighbors overhear things all the time, and maybe she even talked to a few of them. I know that's not all that common nowadays, and she may have tried to avoid people since her apartment is probably the only place where she was able to experience some peace and quiet, but it's still a lead.

"Let's do it," I say before patting the top of my car and getting into the driver's seat.

A fresh surge of energy grips me as I head to West Hollywood to Emilia's luxury apartment building. I roam through the foyer and to the elevator, hitting the button for the top floor operating off my memory. The building had already been canvassed, but I know enough to do multiple sweeps of important places. It's easy to miss something or someone.

"Let's check this one first," Tracie suggests as she motions to the unit closest to the elevator and a few doors down from Emilia's.

She knocks a couple of times before stepping back. We wait a few minutes and knock a few times, but no one answers.

I sigh and place my hands on my hips as I look up and down the hallway, trying to decide which door to try next. It's the middle of the day, so I should expect most people to not answer their doors since they're probably at work.

"That one," I point to the door across the hall. I'm prepared to try on every single door in this hallway and the next if I have to.

Tracie knocks on that one and waits, listening closely.

Thankfully, I can actually hear noise from inside. A few seconds later, the door opens, and a man in his early thirties with wavy blonde hair that falls against his forehead and over his ears appears. He's wearing a white tank top and khaki shorts. He tilts his head out of curiosity, his blue eyes darting from me to Tracie.

"Oh, hello. Can I help you?"

"Detective Carr. Detective Freeman," I gesture to both of us and show my badge, going through the motions. "We wanted to talk to you about your neighbor, Emilia Cruz."

"I'm Chase Romig," he introduces himself as a frown crosses his face. "Yeah, I heard about what happened to her. It's terrible. She was super sweet."

"Can we ask you a few questions, Mr. Romig?" I ask.

"Just call me Chase. Mr. Romig is my dad." Chase shrugs.

"How well did you know her…Chase?"

"Me and my husband have talked to her a handful of times. She wasn't at home a lot because she was so busy, but whenever we came across each other in the hallway, we chatted."

"About what?" Tracie asks.

"Work. Good deals at Whole Foods. That kind of stuff," Chase says.

"Just everyday things? Did she talk about anything or anyone bothering her?" I press him.

Chase thinks for a second before nodding.

"She told us about her ex. I'm guessing that's what you're asking about."

My heart rate spikes. That's exactly the answer I was waiting to hear.

"May we come in? We need to know everything she told you about him."

"Sure," Chase tells me before taking a step back so that we can head into his apartment.

It's tidy and minimalistic with abstract paintings on the wall and decorative throw pillows on the L-shaped, beige couch. He takes a seat on the extended section and joins his hands together, waiting for us to get settled. "Evidently, he had been bothering her a lot after they broke up. Dude wouldn't take a hint."

"Would you say she seemed afraid of him?" Tracie asks.

Chase nods.

"Oh, yeah. Definitely. She blocked him on everything. Phone number. Social media accounts. You name it, she blocked him. But no matter what she did, she never felt fully safe. We felt bad for her. She seemed convinced that he would find her somehow."

I exchange a brief look with Tracie, knowing that she's thinking what I'm thinking.

The more this guy talks, the guiltier Connor looks. Emilia told multiple people about her nervousness toward him. None of these people know a random guy from Iowa, so why would she lie about him? She had no reason to try to garner any sympathy points from anyone.

"Have you seen him around the building? Did he ever try to come to her apartment?" I ask.

"I don't know what he looks like, but I remember seeing some guy in his twenties stop by her place a lot before her…death," Chase shrugs. "But I don't know if it's him. It could've been a friend."

I show him a few photos of Connor from his Instagram account.

Chase shrugs and says, "I don't know. I never got a good look at his face."

I can't think of a guy in his twenties that would be stopping by her place so much. Maybe a cast member, but something tells me that this man could possibly be Connor. If only these hallways had security cameras. It'd be much easier to figure out who was visiting her if this place was monitored.

Tracie glances through her notepad.

"Have you been questioned before? I

would've remembered your statement," she asks.

Chase shakes his head. "No, Jack and I were on a trip when Emilia was found. If any cops came by, we weren't home. I can't really think of anything else that may help, but if you're looking for suspects, her ex-boyfriend is a good place to start."

"Thank you for your time," Tracie says before rising to her feet.

"Of course. I hope you find whoever did this. She didn't deserve it," Chase says as his eyes narrow slightly.

"We will," I assure him before leading Tracie out of his apartment and back out into the hallway. I turn to her and lift my eyebrows in an intrigued manner. "It has to be Connor, right? This aligns with what Emilia was telling everyone."

Tracie doesn't give me the confident nod of agreement I want to see.

"It's possible. He seems like an easy target to pin all of this on, but there are so many other factors to consider. We can't just push them aside until everything is fleshed out and things are set in stone."

A frown almost crosses my face. She's so

rigidly following the rules, never daring to stray even a bit.

I'm not one to rush into decisions, however I'm convinced Connor is behind all of this. Emilia was scared of him and now she's dead.

"I still think we need to look into him more. They have a complicated history, and we need to know if he tried to see her in person when she moved here."

Tracie agrees. "Even if we need to reach out to people from their hometown."

Exploring the past can lend us insight into our current questions. If Connor has exhibited pushy, possessive behavior in the past, it's more likely that he is responsible for Emilia's death.

When Emilia ended their relationship, chances were Connor was not going to take "no" for an answer. Being turned down can be infuriating, leading some to resort to desperate measures.

I can still picture the condition of her body when we discovered it, stomach cut open, her innards spilling out onto the sand. Her face was slack and her lips were slightly open, almost blue in color. Her eyes had dulled to glass as life left them.

"It was an attack filled with malice," I remind her. The image is firmly etched in my memory.

Now more than ever, we have to pick up the pace because it's been days since Emilia's murder. Her killer is actively making moves to distance themselves from her.

"What a case," Tracie sighs as she crosses her arms. "I don't think I've been on one like this before."

I've worked a lot of homicides that were difficult or odd in their own ways, but this one is proving to be the biggest challenge yet. There is so much at play that it's nearly distracting. Sure, it's great that we have multiple leads, but it won't be hard for wires to start getting crossed.

"It probably won't even be the weirdest one you'll encounter in your career," I tell her. "I always swear up and down that the case I'm on is the most difficult only to be proven wrong."

"That's kind of terrifying," Tracie laughs.

I smirk a little and turn toward the door of Emilia's apartment, abruptly pausing at an odd sight. Tracie flashes a confused look.

"I don't remember the caution tape being cut," I say as I point at the yellow tape in front of her door. It's been severed in the middle, leaving her apartment vulnerable. Whoever cuts police tape and breaks into a dead girl's apartment has to be looking for trouble.

And they're about to find what they're looking for.

25

Kaitlyn

In an instant, Tracie and I bolt across the hallway to Emilia's door, getting closer to the tape to quickly inspect it. It's possible that it was torn by accident by a passerby, but when I see how clean the cut is, I know that this is deliberate.

"Looks like it was done with a blade. A sharp one," I say, not seeing any frays or tears except for the initial one.

Tracie nods in agreement, but before she can say anything, a subtle thud sounds from inside of Emilia's apartment. We don't even have to give each other a look before we draw our guns and fall into a ready position. She places her hand over the doorknob as I face the door, prepared to storm in.

I nod and hold my gun out in front of me. The moment she shoves the door open, I charge inside and see a figure bent over in front of a wicker basket near Emilia's entertainment center.

"Hands up! Slowly turn and face me," I order the intruder, seeing Tracie come up on my left side out of the corner of my eye.

The man, who has on a red baseball cap, a black jacket, jeans, and black gloves, puts his hands up and slowly rotates to face us. But when he lifts his head, I realize that he's no stranger.

It's Connor.

"Fancy seeing you here," I say, adrenaline thumping through my head.

What is he doing?

Is he seriously dumb enough to break into her apartment?

"I thought you and Emilia weren't in contact. I hope you know that this is considered trespassing."

"It's not what it seems like," Connor assures me, seeming to stare me down.

I scoff and approach him, keeping my gun trained on him.

"I can't count how many times I've heard that. Hands behind your back."

Connor moves his hands down, joining them together.

"I don't have anything on me," he swears as I start patting him down.

"You cut the tape with something sharp. I doubt you used your teeth," I reply as I check his pants, feeling his phone and wallet.

"There's a small pocketknife on my key ring," Connor admits.

His body is tense. I pitch a quick look behind me to make sure Tracie is between him and the door in case he makes a run for it.

Tracie nods to me.

I pull his keys out and see the knife he mentioned. It's pretty much harmless since its blade is as big as my pinkie, but I still pocket his keys. I take a few steps back and reposition my hands on my gun.

"Why are you here, Connor?" I ask with a stony look on my face. I keep jumping back and forth between him and Elijah because suspicion continuously surrounds them both, but only one of them has been accused of scaring and stalking the deceased.

Connor glances around before sighing.

"Okay, okay… I did see Emilia before she died," he admits. "I hooked up with her a few nights before she died, and I only came back because I left something."

I give him a perplexed look.

"According to multiple sources, she was afraid of you and tried to cut all contact with you. You really expect us to believe that she willingly let you into her apartment?" I ask him, my voice bordering on a scoff.

Does this guy think we're idiots? He's literally wearing gloves! He's up to something shady, and his stiff posture and refusal to look me in the eye for more than two seconds isn't making him seem any more innocent.

"Look, Emilia and I had a complicated relationship. We didn't always get along, and I'm sure she stretched the truth about me because she can get… you know… emotional," Connor says with a shrug and a forced smile. "But there's a part of us that will always love each other. Or did."

"What are you looking for in here? You said you left something," Tracie speaks up from a few feet behind me.

Connor's eyes flick to the side. He sighs slightly, like he knows this is all going wrong, but not knowing how to stop it.

"Oh, nothing important. You know what?

It's probably not even here. I bet it's in my truck. Sorry for the trouble, officers," Connor tells us as he takes a step forward toward the door.

I immediately raise my gun and shout out an order at him to stay where he is and tell me what he was looking for. If it wasn't important, he won't have a problem telling us what it was. What if it isn't his at all?

"Don't move. Tell me what you're looking for," I hiss in his ear. He freezes, his gaze shifting wildly as if searching for any avenue of escape. Trembling, he holds his hands up in surrender knowing that any false move will seal his fate.

"It's… it's just a contact book."

"A what?"

"Address book?" he adds.

I stare at him blankly.

"You know, a place you write down names and numbers and stuff like that."

"Why do you need that? Doesn't your phone work?"

"It's for my…business."

I press him more but he says that he can't say anything else.

With my trigger finger resting on the side of my gun, I consider my choices. If he won't talk then I have no choice but to arrest him for the only thing we have on him. Maybe he'll be more amenable to talk in an interrogation room.

"Turn around. Hands behind your back. You're under arrest for trespassing."

Bewilderment explodes across his face, and for a moment, it looks like he's about to say something. However, he shuts his mouth as I read him his rights.

Tracie handcuffs him as I watch him closely, wondering if there's any truth behind the item being an address book. Who even has one of those anymore?

We take him down to my car and put him in the back where a cage separates the front seat and backseat. I shut him inside before stepping a few feet away with Tracie.

"I don't believe a word that comes out of his mouth," I shake my head. He's already lied directly to our faces, so I know that I can't trust him.

"He's definitely hiding something," Tracie agrees. "Don't people just put their contacts into their phones nowadays?"

"That's what I was thinking. After we process him, we need to do some more searching on our own. Maybe we'll find this so-called contact book," I say, crossing my arms over my chest.

"Or we'll find nothing at all," Tracie hisses under her breath, her eyes narrowing. "Maybe he was just snooping, some people get a strange joy out of rummaging through dead people's possessions like they're souvenirs."

I glance over at Connor, who is deep in thought.

"I think it's more than that for him. I think there's actually something in there that he was looking for, and I want to make sure we find it first."

Tracie nods.

On the drive to the station, my eyes dart up to the rear-view mirror occasionally only to see Connor staring back at me. I don't care if it takes me all night. I'm going to find out what he's hiding from me.

26

Kaitlyn

The cell door creaks as it swings shut behind Connor, locking him in one of the jail cells that we use as a drunk tank. He's not intoxicated but I need to keep him somewhere safe so that we can have time to go through the apartment. If this contact book does indeed exist, maybe there's something in there that can help us with our investigation.

"I'm just glad we finally have a suspect to question," Tracie says when I meet her in the lobby. "It may not actually mean anything, but it feels like one step closer to solving this."

I want to wrap this case up for Emilia. Her name is on every headline. Her smiling face is everywhere from morning shows to the evening news and bloggers' websites. People are speculating and spreading rumors left and right, and I'm ready to put this all to rest. Everyone deserves the truth, Emilia included.

I'm ready to put *her* to rest.

"I guess we'll see. It depends on what's in Emilia's apartment and what Connor is willing to tell us," I say.

If he's smart, he'll demand a lawyer and keep his mouth shut. We don't have much to keep him on besides the trespassing charge and he'll likely walk unless we find something else.

Tracie nods before we go out to my car and make the drive back to Emilia's apartment building. I make sure to bring some extra police tape so that I can seal the door off again after we're done.

"I'll check in her bedroom," Tracie offers once we're inside.

"I'll look around the living room," I say before we split up. My eyes sweep over the living room as I walk farther into the space, soon catching sight of a small bookcase with a few accent pieces on top like a ceramic seashell and a white block sign that has 'Escape the Ordinary' in swirly, gold lettering.

I crouch down and start browsing through the books neatly lined up on the three shelves.

Novels. Self-help. Acting manuals. Nothing out of the ordinary and nothing that resembles a contact book.

I look through every shelf and then see that a few books on the bottom are jutting out of line slightly. I push on them to nudge them back into place, but they don't budge. Something is behind them.

I draw in a sharp breath as I pull them out, revealing a black Moleskin notebook pressed flush against the back of the bookcase.

Like someone was trying to hide it!

After putting on gloves, I grab it and straighten up, my fingertips brushing over the smooth cover. It's slightly worn, definitely used. I flip through the pages to see that a lot of them have been written on.

"Tracie!" I call out as my heart starts racing. "I may have found what Connor was looking for."

"What is it?" She hurries into the living room.

I hold up the notebook to show her.

"I think this may be Connor's," I say as I show her a page that's been written on. The handwriting isn't precise or swirly. It's essentially chicken scratch that's hastily written.

Tracie shrugs and nods a little.

"Looks kind of like my son's handwriting," she laughs.

I point to the empty spot on the shelf.

"I found it hidden behind there," I say, seeing her eyebrows shoot up with interest.

Tracie moves to stand by my side so we can both read.

The page has three columns. The first column has names, but not normal ones. Hoops, Blondie, and Romeo.

Who knows who these nicknames belong to? My forefinger moves to the next column, which lists amounts in what looks like pounds and grams. A heavy feeling grows in my stomach as I look at the other column, which lists various amounts of money.

The header reads 'Money Owed' in all caps.

"Drugs. It has to be drugs," Tracie says.

I nod in agreement.

"This has to be Connor," I reply as I flip through some more pages, seeing more columns of nicknames and numbers. There are a lot of sales in this book, which means a lot of drugs. I don't even know what specifically is being sold yet.

"But that means he was actually here," Tracie points out.

"Doesn't mean she invited him in. He could've broken in here. Again," I say, wanting to explore all possibilities. Unfortunately, we don't know exactly how this notebook showed up, but I know someone who can tell us.

Tracie rubs her temple as she lets out a slow breath.

"Just when I think things are smoothing out…" she murmurs.

That's just the nature of law enforcement. Nothing is as it seems, and I'm always prepared for a curveball.

Granted, I definitely didn't expect this.

"Lots of drugs in this case," I mutter as I shut the notebook. "I think that's all we need from here. It has to be what he's looking for."

"It's kind of a contact book."

I scoff a little as we head out of Emilia's apartment, holding the notebook close to my chest. We had already filled out the evidence sheet, logging exactly where and when we found it and signing our names. This is a huge piece of evidence for us, so I'm not letting it out of my sight.

After shutting the door, I tape it off and take

a step back, peering at her apartment and wondering when it would be cleaned out and rented by someone else.

Will it be disclosed that Emilia used to live here?

Would the next renter even care?

I don't know if I could live in the place of someone who had been murdered. All I'd be able to think about is that they left their house one day and never returned home.

I feel a strange mix of emotions when it comes to my job. There's an underlying dread that I can never shake, no matter how much I try. Death is something that I have to face on a daily basis, and it takes its toll both physically and mentally. I try not to become too attached to any one case, but the lives that are taken hit me hard. It's a cycle of guilt and grief, but I try to remain stoic.

Glancing over at Tracie, I take a deep breath and push all of that away. "Let's get back to the station. I want to get a confession out of him."

27

Kaitlyn

"Comfortable?" I ask as we sit at a table across from Connor in the interrogation room. I doubt he finds my sarcasm charming.

He sits stiffly in his chair, his eyes darting back and forth between me and Tracie. Keeping his arms crossed tightly over his chest, I can see the tension in his jaw as he clenches and unclenches it.

Tracie leans forward, her eyes fixed on his face. "We need to know what happened, Connor," she says in a calm, measured tone.

Connor's eyes narrow, and he is struggling to keep his emotions in check. "I already told you everything," he growls. "I don't know anything else."

I exchange a look with Tracie, and then lean back in my chair.

"Listen, Connor," I say, adopting a softer tone. "We know this is a difficult situation for you. But we need to know what happened."

Connor's eyes flicker with something that looks like fear, and you can see the sweat starting to bead on his forehead. "I...I don't know," he stammers.

Tracie leans forward again, her voice firm.

"We don't think you did anything, Connor," she lies. "But we need to know what happened. Every detail could be important. We went back to Emilia's apartment and found something interesting."

Tracie rests her hands on the surface of the table, intertwining her fingers.

Connor's stony expression wavers. If I had to guess, his mouth probably went dry too. His eyes dart between us yet he remains silent.

I place the black notebook, which has been carefully stored in an evidence bag, on the table between us, watching his eyes widen and his shoulders fall slightly. "Recognize this?"

Connor averts his gaze and adopts a nonchalant posture by leaning back in his chair.

However, his demeanor fails to deceive me as I can tell that he is on the verge of breaking into a sweat. He has been caught with something that contains evidence of his involvement in drug transactions.

"I don't know. I've seen a lot of black notebooks."

I nearly laugh. Is he seriously playing dumb right now? I know he hasn't made the smartest decisions today, but he's not an idiot.

"Connor, you've already lied to us before. I suggest you make things easier on yourself and be truthful," I say in a firm voice, planting my hands on the table as I lean forward slightly.

Connor looks over at Tracie, who merely gives him a stern expression. If he's looking for the 'good cop' between the two of us, he's out of luck. We both want his confession.

"It… kind of looks familiar," he caves, staring at the table.

With a gloved hand, I open the bag and slip the notebook out, feeling his eyes digging into me. I open the notebook and show him a page.

"This is your handwriting, right?" I press.

Connor glances up briefly, but he doesn't take the time to actually inspect it before answering.

"Yeah, looks like it," he murmurs quietly. It's a mistake on his part to admit something like that to me. It would be in his best interest to stay quiet and say nothing but he hasn't asked for a lawyer even though I made him well aware of his right to do so. Whatever mistakes he makes now will be his to live with and to our benefit.

"You know, these names and numbers are really interesting," I say, tapping the columns with my index finger. "Kind of seems like transactions of something that's measured in pounds and grams."

Connor's face starts to get flushed. A few beads of sweat gather at the temples. He swallows hard.

"It's just product," his voice tight and stiff.

"What kind of product?" Tracie asks.

Connor sighs and hangs his head a little.

"Okay, look… I do sell some drugs. They're so much cheaper here than in Iowa, and we need the money," he confesses, the words spilling out of him.

There it is. Come on out with it, I say silently to myself. Now, how much of this did Emilia know?

"Why?" Tracie asks as she starts writing

down notes, despite the conversation being recorded. "Why do you need the money?"

Connor sinks back in his seat.

"To save my family's farm. It's all they have, and they had a big balloon payment to make. No matter how hard they tried, they couldn't come up with enough money, so I took matters into my own hands. Emilia helped connect me with some people in L.A., so I started selling around here to make a better profit. Pills are still expensive in Iowa, mostly because they're harder to get."

"She knew that you were selling drugs?" I ask.

Connor shrugs.

"She told me that she didn't want to know what I was up to. She didn't explicitly hook me up with drug dealers. She just gave me some names of people she knew from her friends. Through them, I was able to get what I needed."

I drum my fingers against the surface of the table as I think. Some things still don't add up. This is her ex-boyfriend, the one she was supposedly trying to get away from.

"And that's the extent of your interaction with Emilia? You asked her for help?"

Connor shakes his head.

"Like I said before, we hooked up, too. Just a few days before she was killed," he sighs. "I reached out to her the next day, and she never got back to me."

I glance over at Tracie, who is hastily jotting down a bunch of notes. We need to revisit the timeline we've been drawing out to see if any of this can be substantiated with phone records.

"We heard she blocked you on social media, your phone, everything," I say.

Connor nods.

"I don't know. Maybe someone else did. But that was the last time I saw her."

I narrow my eyes and lean forward, holding his gaze.

"You didn't see her on the day she died? You didn't kill her to tie up loose ends since she knew you were up to no good?" My accusations come out sharply.

Astonishment fills his face as he leans back away from me.

"What? I didn't kill her!" he protests. "I would never hurt her!"

Tracie puts her hand up to get him to calm down and lower his voice.

"The two of you had a rocky relationship.

You became involved in illegal activities, and she knew about it. You must've known that she talked badly about you. That didn't make you mad?" she asks.

Connor shakes his head.

"No! I know how she felt about me, but that didn't affect how I felt about her. When I found out she died, I… I couldn't even believe it at first. She was in my life forever, and the thought of her just being… gone… crushed me. It still crushes me!" he says, his eyes gleaming slightly.

"You had feelings for her that she didn't return," I state.

Connor nods as he releases a shaky breath, sweat beading on his forehead.

"Yeah, but I didn't kill her. Or hurt her. Or stalk her. I was sad about it and hoped that we would get back together, but she made it clear that she wasn't interested. When she didn't get back to me after we slept together, I was prepared to give it up for good."

I grind my teeth for a few seconds, listening to the scratching of Tracie's pen against the paper. I'm not sure that I believe him. Her sleeping with him again would be a sign that maybe she was interested. Unless, that's a lie, too.

I wanna keep digging and poke around to see if there are any holes in his story. Maybe there's something he hasn't mentioned yet that could expose him. Given his propensity for deception, it's possible that there exists a discrepancy in his account that could uncover the real truth.

"You broke into her apartment today," I say.

Connor waves his hands in a dismissive manner.

"Just to get my notebook back. I'm sure my fingerprints are on it, and I didn't want it to be found to tie me to my drug business," he admits as he looks me in the eye. "That's it. I swear."

I continue to eye him. He was rummaging around quite a lot.

Wouldn't he know exactly where it was? Maybe. Or maybe Emilia moved it. Maybe the reason she never got back to him was that she wanted him out of this life and didn't want him to keep selling drugs.

"Why not keep your records on your phone?" I ask.

Connor glares at me with a look of disbelief.

"Because everything on a phone can be tracked. It's too risky. As long as you don't lose it, paper is the safest way to store something."

"Well, you lost it," I tell him as I tuck the notebook back into the evidence bag.

Connor's shoulders slouch. Tracie and I are exhausted, too. It's a small comfort to finally have someone in the interrogation room, but his story hasn't given us much when it comes to her death.

"I didn't kill her," Connor says, leaning over the table. "You have to believe me."

Tracie places her notepad in her lap before peering at him. "Where were you that Sunday, the night of the 23rd?"

Connor thinks for a moment before perking up and nodding quickly.

"Yeah, she went to that award show and still hadn't gotten back to me at that point. I was feeling pretty sorry for myself and hopeless about us, so… I went to a strip club. It's not something I do often, but I went that night because I didn't want to be alone at the Airbnb."

"What club?" Tracie asks, her pen poised above her note page.

"Spearmint Rhino," Connor says, rubbing the back of his neck sheepishly. "I'm pretty sure they have cameras there, so you'll see me there. I stayed until like midnight."

“Where did you go after that?” I ask.

The room is silent, save for the gentle whir of the ceiling fan spinning lazily above us. I sit across from him, Tracie’s pen hovering expectantly as we await an answer. His shoulders are tense, and he nervously runs his hands through his hair. He clears his throat just as he’s about to speak.

"After the club, I didn't really have a plan," his voice was soft, almost inaudible. "I knew I had to get away from all of this, so I just got in my car. I ended up back at my rental after driving around for a bit.”

He paused, and I waited for him to continue. Finally, he looks up at me, his gaze unreadable. “That's where I was. All night. Maybe there’s a traffic camera on that street.”

“I need the address,” Tracie says.

While Connor looks it up on her phone, I peer at him silently, noting the tension in his shoulders and the restlessness of his eyes. Even after years on the job, it’s still hard to tell if someone is lying. And it’s particularly hard to tell if someone is lying just *a little bit.*

“The more you cooperate, the better things will be for you,” I remind him getting up to my feet.

This isn't exactly true. It would have been in his best interest to not talk to us at all and wait for his attorney.

But this isn't about *his* best interest.

28

Kaitlyn

On the drive over to the *Spearmint Rhino,* I text with Luke who has already left for Sacramento. With everything that I have to deal with during the day, seeing him after work and in the mornings grounds me. It helps me stay strong and focused and I'm really going to miss him.

"You okay?" Tracie's voice drags me out of my thoughts.

I give her a slight nod. The closer we get, the seedier the area becomes. As we make our way down the dimly lit street, the sounds of blaring music and drunken laughter echo through the air. The neon lights of the nearby strip club flash, casting a warm glow. Despite the luxurious exterior of the club, the buildings lining the street are dilapidated and rundown, with boarded-up storefronts and cracked pavement. The smell of stale alcohol and cigarette smoke hangs heavily in the air, mixing with the scent of garbage and decay.

I find a parking spot and we make our way past groups of disheveled and intoxicated individuals huddled in corners, their faces etched with exhaustion and despair. The alleys and side streets are dark and foreboding, with only the occasional flicker of a streetlamp to illuminate the way.

The strip club itself is a gaudy monstrosity, with flashing lights and a garish sign. It's a place that seems to exist outside of time, a world unto itself. I can't help but feel a sense of unease. The unhoused people who live outside are living in a reality where survival means doing whatever it takes, no matter the cost. I can't help but wonder what will become of them, trapped in this never-ending cycle of poverty and desperation.

My thoughts return to Emilia and the Order. High-profile cases usually make big waves, and all I have to do is follow the chaos until I find my suspect. But the hardest part of it all is finding the proof I need to convict them.

It doesn't matter what I know. What matters is what I can prove in court.

"Everything okay?" Tracie asks.

"Yep, just thinking about Luke," I lie.

"He's gone, right? For FBI training?" Her face softens.

"To Sacramento."

"I'm sure he'll enjoy it."

"Not really. He barely wants to be in the FBI anymore," I murmur.

Tracie's eyebrows rise in surprise.

"Really? All I hear about is people trying to get into the academy. The FBI is the big leagues."

I crack a dry smile.

"It's not for everyone though. He's getting pretty tired of it and wants to do something else. Something different."

Tracie nods in understanding.

"You ever think about trying something new?" she asks.

I immediately shake my head without even having to think about my answer. I don't know who I'd be if I weren't a detective. Sure, there's more to my life than just work, but I feel like I was always meant to do this job. To hunt down the bad guys. To seek justice.

It makes sense to me.

"No, what about you? You went to the police academy a bit later in life. What made you want to do that?"

"Same thing as you. Plus, sitting in an office wasn't for me. I wanted to be part of the action. Solving cases like this, it's something to be proud of."

"And if we don't?" I ask, playing the devil's advocate.

"We'll just keep going until we do," she says, but I know that it's not that easy. Sometimes, cases just reach dead ends.

But this one doesn't exactly feel like it will. Between the overdose that might be a murder, a drug operation, and a cult, we have a lot of angles to pursue.

"First, let's figure out if Connor's alibi holds up." I sigh and walk toward the strip club. "Let's track down the manager."

I'm secretly hoping that he's not the type to not give us the time of day. But I know that people who run these types of establishments tend to get defensive. They don't want cops prying into their business.

Tracie nods and motions for me to lead the way.

I walk up to the glass door and pull it open, hearing the rhythmic thump of dance music as it echoes throughout the club. Despite the colorful lights shining on circular platforms for dancers to spin around poles on and a runway for them to strut down, it's dark inside. I can make out a bar to the right, and there's a balcony on the second floor that overlooks the main stage. I guess the top floor is the VIP area for private dances.

"I don't even know where to look," I admit, my eyes moving over customers sitting at tables and lounges near the platforms and the runway as they admire the dancers with cash in their hands. Multiple dollar bills already litter the floor at the dancers' feet as they sway their hips and wrap around the silver poles in thongs and pasties.

"Should we ask one of them?" Tracie suggests as she points to the nearest platform where an old man throws a twenty on the stage in front of a blonde.

"Why not?"

It's too dark to find any sort of office door, and I don't want to waste time scouring the place that's fairly big for a strip club.

Tracie follows me up to the circular stage,

lifting her hand to capture the dancer's attention.

The blonde walks to the edge of the platform and leans down, her cleavage becoming even more noticeable in her lacy, red bra.

"Hi there," she purrs, thinking we're just customers. The moment we show our badges, her smile morphs into a nervous frown. "Oh."

I put up my badge and shake my head.

"We just want to know where your manager is," I tell her.

The blonde turns and points at the back left corner.

"Gary's office is there."

"Thanks," I reply before heading that way, noticing how the customers seem to shrink back in their chairs as I walk by. It's like they think I'm going to arrest them for being at a strip club.

The office door is closed and I knock a few times until a man in his forties with a noticeable beer gut and thinning black hair opens it.

"What is it?" He growls.

I already have my badge ready.

"We need to speak with you about taking a look at your security footage," I say. "It's for an important case."

"What kind of case?" Gary scrunches his forehead.

"We need to see if someone was actually here on the night of a murder," I say, not beating around the bush. I need him to be more accommodating.

"If he says he was here, he was here. Usually, people try to cover up the fact that they were in a place like this," Gary says in a dismissive manner before retreating into his office.

I slam my hand against the door to keep him from closing it, fixing him with a hard stare.

"Your cooperation would be greatly appreciated," I say through my gritted teeth.

Gary's eyes widen and he glares, crossing his arms over his chest.

"If you want the footage, I want to see a warrant," he states with a snide tone.

Son of a bitch. It is within his right to demand that, but why does he have to be so damn difficult? He was making my job harder. I held his glare and tightened my fingers into fists, wishing he would change his mind.

"Can you at least tell me if you saw this man here on the night of the 23rd?" I show him a photo of Connor.

He looks at it carefully, shakes his head and then gives me a shrug.

"We have a lot of people come through here."

"That's why I'd like to see your footage."

"Then get a warrant. And don't bother my dancers. They're working."

I clench my jaw. Tracie leans closer.

"Come on. Let's go," she says.

I force myself to turn away from Gary, cussing him out silently as Tracie leads me away. Before we can go back the way we came, I nudge her and lead her along the back wall, wanting to get a good look at the place. I didn't have any footage to go off of, but I wanted to see if there were enough cameras to even help us in the first place.

"Camera toward the entrance. The bar. The stages," I murmur.

"But not toward that door. Looks like a back exit," Tracie says as she gestures toward the door in the back right of the club.

"Of course," I mutter before looking up at the balcony on the second floor. I highly doubt there is a single camera up there, which means we're flat out of luck.

"What now?" Tracie sighs looking around aimlessly.

I shake my head as frustration claws through me in a fiery wave. It only takes one person to create a roadblock in this case.

"Let's get out of here."

29

Kaitlyn

After leaving the strip club, Tracie and I find ourselves at a mom-and-pop sandwich shop. I don't have much of an appetite, but I haven't eaten all day. Plus, Tracie and I need a place to sit down and talk about what we're going to do next. Our one lead fell through, and we have no other way to confirm that Connor wasn't lying about being at the *Spearmint Rhino* on the night of Emilia's death.

I eat my club sandwich and potato chips on autopilot, working through a bunch of failed options and suggestions for our next move. I don't want to double back too much since we have gotten so far with just a few leads, but all I see are roadblocks. More and more roadblocks.

"It'll take a while to get a warrant," Tracie says as she picks around at her Cobb salad with her plastic fork.

I shake my head, putting my sandwich down, my stomach churning in protest. I'm just not in the mood to eat right now. There's too much on my mind, and when my mind is busy, my stomach prefers to stay empty.

"Forget it. We need to move on," I say, resting my hands on top of the white, square table.

"What about Connor? This was supposed to tell us if he's a prime suspect, " Tracie asks looking confused.

I sigh and shrug.

"We either believe him or not. Maybe Gary was right. If he said he was there, he was probably there. Why say your alibi is a strip club?" I point out.

I don't want it to make sense because there is still a chance that Connor may be the murderer, but it's hard to argue for that when there's no evidence to substantiate it. Sure, we have fingerprints on a notebook, and him admitting to certain things, but that's not enough.

Things like this are the most frustrating parts of the job.

"He could still be lying about what he did after he went to the strip club. Maybe he didn't go back to his Airbnb and went to find Emilia instead," Tracie suggests as she puts down her fork.

That's always a possibility. He may still be lying, but we're facing a dead end at this point when it comes to him.

"We don't have anything to hold him on," I sigh. "Not for long. It's just trespassing."

Tracie frowns in disappointment.

"Not even the notebook?" she asks. "He broke into her apartment!"

I can hardly believe my next words.

"Selling drugs isn't necessarily evidence of murder. Besides, I believe him."

"You do? I thought you were convinced that he's the one who killed Emilia," Tracie questions me. "I mean, it's not a long shot. When you hear hoof beats, think horses not zebras."

Because it's likely for boyfriends and husbands or ex-partners to be involved in the murder of a woman.

The wires in my brain feel all twisted up. Connor is a possible suspect, but it feels like we've hardly scratched the surface when it comes to Elijah and the Order. I want to hit all of my bases.

I'm not sloppy. I can be impulsive, but I won't be when charging someone with murder.

"We need more evidence. The only reason that notebook is in there is because she let him in," I point out.

"But she's afraid of him," Tracie says.

I shrug, not able to come up with an answer for that. People are hard to read when you delve down deep. They turn out to be so much different than I expected. From what I heard, Emilia didn't want to be anywhere near Connor. She seemed wary of him.

But she let him into her apartment. She let him stay long enough for him to leave things there. It doesn't make sense to me, but I only know Emilia through people who know her and through what she's put out on social media.

"I don't know, Tracie. Maybe she had a lapse of judgment. Got caught up in her old feelings. Those types of things happen. She might have regretted it afterward and didn't reach out to him again."

Tracie sighs, seeming to deflate on the spot.

She shakes her head and leans it against her hand as she props her elbow up on the table.

"It felt like we were close," she murmurs. "I thought we finally had him."

"But what do we have really? I mean, in actual evidence?"

I can hear the frustration in her voice. Not only is this case wearing on her professionally, but I'm sure it's keeping her away from her family more than she likes. Cases like these are tough to deal with all around, and I'm not sure if we're close to the end.

Even if I felt convinced that Connor is the murderer, I have no evidence of that. We're still stuck in place, and the direction for us to go next is unclear.

"We may still be," I say, wanting to lift her spirits. I can't drag around a pessimistic partner. "But we need to figure out another angle to tackle."

Silence lingers between us for a minute until my phone starts ringing, prompting me to grab it and stand from the table.

"Just a second," I tell Tracie before stepping out of the sandwich shop and standing on the sidewalk. I hit the answer button and put my phone against my ear. "Kaitlyn Carr."

"Hello, Detective. You told me to call you if I had any more findings regarding Emilia Cruz."

I immediately recognize Dr. Laura Berinsky's voice, the medical examiner on Emilia's case. I had been meaning to reach out since it had been radio silence for a while.

"What have you found?" I ask, my heart rate ticking up.

"As you remember, her body had sustained a lot of damage. Most of her intestines were on the outside."

The image of Emilia's body laid out on the beach, her organs spilling free, flashes through my mind. The animalistic act makes my stomach churn.

Was it fueled by hate? Or was there some other reason?

"Of course." My words sound stiff.

"It might have been a cover up."

My eyes grow wide as I take a step farther away from the sandwich shop.

"For what?" I press.

"Her liver was removed. Quite carefully and strategically it seems," Laura says.

"No way," I whisper.

Why would someone do that? I wonder.

Could it have been a botched surgery? A desperate attempt at black-market organ trafficking? Or perhaps something more sinister, like a sadistic killer looking to collect a gruesome trophy?

"It could have been taken for a medical transplant," Laura suggests. "Especially when it's something like the liver or the kidneys."

"Is anything else missing?"

"No, just her liver. Kidneys are intact, along with everything else."

A lot of people are on the transplant list to get a new liver, but why take Emilia's?

"Did you find anything else?"

Laura pauses for a moment before speaking. I hear the noise of papers rustling in the background.

"Yes, it's not 100%, but it looks like Emilia's body was most likely tossed overboard from a boat instead of being left on the shore."

"Did she have a lot of water in her lungs?" I ask, wondering how she drew that conclusion.

"No, not at all. She was killed somewhere else. Not only that, but there's evidence of her being eaten by fish and other water scavengers. When people are dumped on the shore, we don't see evidence of scavenging on the bodies.

Whoever threw her overboard probably didn't think she'd wash up eventually."

"Any evidence of any restraints or anything that they could have attached to her to keep her down?"

"No, I doubt they weighed her down with anything at all."

Things wash up on the beach all the time. Trash, clothes, shells. Bodies are rare, but it definitely happens. The few bodies that I have seen turn up had ropes around their wrists and ankles attached to cement blocks, which got caught on something and broke free.

I thank her for her time and tell her that I'll be in touch.

I have to interpret a lot from this information to make it useful and have it point me in the right direction, but it's one of the biggest clues we've gotten for this case. The reason for Emilia's death is her liver.

Who wanted her liver?

I lower the phone from my ear as I stare ahead at the street in front of me, cars passing. They have no idea that Emilia Cruz's liver was expertly removed.

Why? Where is it now? In someone else's body?

A pang echoes in my stomach as I step away from the street, grounding myself before poking my head into the sandwich shop. I wave my hand to catch Tracie's attention, and she gives me a perplexed look.

"Come on. We've got a lead."

30

Kaitlyn

"You've got to be joking," Tracie gasps.

An electric, excited grin crosses my face as I watch her reaction. We sit in my car across the street from the sandwich shop, not wanting anyone to hear our conversation. This is a huge development, and I know we have to do more work to try to figure out who would want Emilia's liver.

"I couldn't believe it when she told me. I thought all of her organs were intact, but her insides were a mess," I shake my head in disbelief.

Tracie thinks for a moment before her eyes dart to mine.

"Do you think this is some sort of black market operation? What if we've been delving into her personal life and this case isn't even… personal? What if it's random?"

I highly doubt this is random since Emilia is so widely known, but I suppose weirder things have happened. It could always be a case of wrong place and wrong time. Maybe she left the after-party, took a walk, and ran into a psycho looking for a good liver. Maybe then this person sold it on the black market for thousands of dollars.

"It's possible," I say. "She definitely wouldn't be selling her own organs. I know some people get desperate enough to sell a kidney or something when they're in the hole, but no one can live without their liver."

"They can give up a lobe, but it sounds like the whole thing is gone," Tracie replies with a thoughtful look on her face, her eyebrows knitting together. "But why her liver?"

"That's what I've been asking myself. If it's a black market sort of thing, why go after a celebrity who's harder to get to? Why not a homeless person or someone who wouldn't be missed?" I ask as my eyes drift up to the rearview mirror.

I can see the creases in my forehead get deeper as my pupils dilate.

The liver is gone, who knows where it is. I can't track an organ, and I don't know who took it out. If it's been expertly removed, is a doctor involved?

The person who removed her liver had to have done it before.

"If it's for the black market, they would have taken other things too," Tracie says thinking out loud. "They had every opportunity to take all of her organs, but they didn't."

A sigh breaks from me when I realize that she's most likely right. So, where does that even leave us?

"Maybe we should look through some records and see if there have been any other murders with missing livers in the past year?"

Tracie shrugs.

"I'm not sure how helpful that will be though. She's not just anybody."

"It has to be someone who knows her," I murmur to myself. I can't think of a reason for anyone who knows her to take her liver. "Her just being murdered made more sense than this."

Tracie nods in agreement.

"Just another confusing layer to an already complicated case," she sighs.

Silence falls between us as I check the time. The day has flown by, and it's already evening. I've been up for hours, and I need some rest. At this point, my brain is filled with a cloudy haze, and it's getting harder to piece things together. I'm useless when exhausted.

"Let's call it a day," I suggest.

Tracie gives me a surprised look. Usually, she's the one wrapping things up.

"That's probably a good idea. We'll get started early in the morning."

I nod in agreement and turn on my car. I take us back to the station and grab my things from inside, meeting Tracie in the lobby.

"See you tomorrow," I say.

Tracie gives me a small smile.

"We're going to figure this out. Any day now," she assures me.

I want to believe her. It'll be nice to throw someone behind bars.

"What if the liver was taken just to confuse us?" I ask.

Tracie gives me a pointed look.

"Get some rest, Kaitlyn," she heads out of the station.

A sigh breaks from me as I massage my temples, knowing I need to follow her advice.

Why would someone take an organ without trying to sell it? Obviously, whoever did this didn't mean for the body to be found.

I get in my car and drive home to a dark, empty house, my heart aching when I'm once again reminded that Luke is gone. I want to talk to him and have him take my mind off things. He's the only one who can.

I chew on my bottom lip as I look down at my phone, bringing up our messages.

Want to FaceTime?

I send it off before changing into one of his t-shirts and a pair of pajama shorts, my back hitting the bed as I flop down onto it. My body immediately aches before relaxing, my exhaustion seeming to sink into my bones. I love my job, but I wish I had some vacation days left to get my mind off this for a little bit.

I haven't felt this exhausted in a while.

When my phone goes off, I sit up and grab it, seeing the incoming FaceTime screen pop up.

I cross my legs and answer, Luke's tired face appears on the screen.

"Hey," I say as a smile crosses my lips.

"Hey, baby," Luke murmurs as he lays on his hotel bed, grinning up at the camera. "I miss you."

My heart throbs as I gaze at his face, taking in his features that I've studied over and over again. I wish he were here with me right now, but this is the best we can do until his training is finally over.

"I miss you. How's everything going?" I ask, wanting him to tell me every detail and get my mind off work.

Luke groans as he rolls onto his back, holding his phone above his head so that I can get a peek at his bare chest.

"It's so boring. I feel like I've done all of this before," he says. "It's unnecessary."

I frown a little, hearing how tired he is of it all. He wants to do something different so badly, and if that makes him happy, I'm all for it. Life is short, right? There's no point spending time doing something that doesn't satisfy him.

"We should seriously look for something different for you."

Luke's face softens.

"Yeah?" he asks.

I smile and nod.

"Of course. Maybe we can figure something out after the wedding," I suggest.

That's coming up very quickly. Luckily, I've pretty much gotten everything taken care of except for a few small things. Luke is quite happy about that as well. Before we know it, we'll be in Malibu.

Luke smiles back, awe gleaming in his eyes.

"I love you," he tells me. "I can't wait to see you."

"Only a few more days," I remind him as we warmly gaze at each other, my body feeling lighter now. "And I love you. A lot."

A slightly worried expression fills his eyes.

"Are you doing okay? How's the case going?"

I look away from the screen, not even knowing where to start. Maybe I don't even want to.

"It's… crazy. I don't think I've ever worked on something like this before, Luke."

He sits up, concerned. "I hope you're taking it easy and getting some sleep. You can get pretty… involved."

"Obsessed?" I cock an eyebrow at him, knowing that's what he meant.

Luke chuckles.

"You're just really determined. I don't want you to neglect basic necessities because you're focusing on the case too much."

I suppose I can't blame him for worrying about me. I don't take it easy. I don't stop and breathe. All I know is to go, go, go because that's what gets things done. Being passive is torturous to me, and I'm marrying one of the most relaxed people on the planet.

Opposites certainly do attract.

"I'm okay," I assure him. "I'm just ready to find this guy and send it off to the prosecutor's office."

"It's coming. You're the most capable person I know," Luke replies with a warm look on his face.

I smirk a little as I move to lay down on my side, tilting the camera to keep my face in view.

"I think you feel obligated to say that."

"Not at all," he smiles crossing his heart with his forefinger. "You're amazing, Kaitlyn."

Warmth blooms on my face as I shake my head. He's the sweetest guy I know, and I'm lucky to have him. I'm aware that I'm not the most laid back, easygoing person, but he doesn't seem to care in the slightest.

"I really wish you were here."

The bed feels too big without him in it with me.

Luke's eyebrows pop up as a flirty grin crosses his face.

"Oh, yeah? What would you do if I were?" he asks in his best low, sultry voice.

Laughter bursts from me.

"Are we horny teenagers or something?" I reply as I give him an amused look.

Luke shrugs.

"Soon to be newlyweds. We can act like some if you want," he says as he shoots me a wink.

I smirk and shake my head. I can't even remember the last time we had phone sex. But both of our eyelids flutter and I know that we're too tired to delve into something like that right now. I wouldn't mind the real thing when he gets back home, though.

"I'm sure you'd rather watch one of your boring history documentaries. Which one are you on now?" I tease.

He's such a history nerd, but it's one of the many things that I love about him. If there's a documentary to watch, he's going to binge it until the very end. Luckily, most hotel televisions have the History Channel.

"Wow, am I that predictable?" Luke laughs sitting up. "I did actually start one, though."

Of course.

"What's it about?" I ask, admiring the smooth planes of his built chest as he shifts the camera.

"It's pretty weird. It delves into the occult in 19th century England. There were a lot of spiritualistic movements and a rise in cults."

"We've got some today," I can't help but smirk.

"Not like these. They're super hardcore," Luke replies with a little laugh. "We're talking sacrifices. Removing organs."

I immediately sit straight up, my heartbeat echoing in my head.

"Removing organs?" I ask to make sure I heard him right.

Luke nods, his eyes on the television.

"Yeah, these people think the liver is like some sort of repository of spiritual essence in the body. It's crazy," he chuckles.

Spiritual essence! Why didn't I tie this to a ritual? She's literally involved in a group all about spirituality and wellness. I pegged them as a bit extreme but are they crazy enough to remove someone's liver? That definitely wasn't in the welcome letter.

"Luke, I'm sorry, but I have to go. I think you helped me find a break in the case," I say, adrenaline coursing through me and making my fingertips turn to ice. It's too late to do anything but research on the internet.

Tomorrow, though, I know what to do. Finally, there's a direction for me to move in, and I'm *running*.

"That's what I'm here for," Luke chuckles. "I love you."

"Love you!" I say before ending the call.

A fresh jolt of motivation strikes me like lightning, and I don't feel an ounce of exhaustion anymore. I wish Tracie was up so that I could tell her, but there's no need for both of us to be losing sleep. It can wait until tomorrow.

31

Kaitlyn

The sun beats down on the asphalt as I merge onto U.S. Highway 101. The traffic is heavy, with cars whizzing past me in both directions. The landscape changes quickly as I leave the city behind. Tall buildings give way to rolling hills, dotted with farms and vineyards.

As we drive, I can't help but feel a sense of anticipation. I don't know what we'll find when we get to our destination, but I know that it's important. Tracie sits next to me, watching the scenery fly by.

The road stretches out before us, a ribbon of concrete that winds through the hills and valleys. We pass through small towns and bustling cities, each with their own unique charm. As we drive, the miles tick by, and I feel myself getting closer to the answers I seek.

"Will you tell me where we're going now?" Tracie asks as she holds a cup of coffee from the gas station.

I didn't even let her enter the police station before I dragged her to my car, telling her we needed to hit the road and that I'd explain on the way.

I glance over at her and give a small smile.

"Santa Barbara. We're going to Elijah's mansion," I tell her as I merge over into the left lane, speeding up to whip past the slower cars. Technically, there's no need for me to be in a hurry since Elijah doesn't know we're coming, but I want to get there as soon as possible. I need to pry a little more into the group's practices to see just how far they're willing to go to reach enlightenment.

Tracie pitches me a confused look.

"What? Why? Did you find something out? It's only been a night!"

That's the thing about me. It doesn't matter if it's three in the morning or eleven at night. If I'm determined to get work done, I'm getting it done.

"Nothing is concrete, but we need more answers."

If we're going to find any, it'll be at the mansion. I tell her about the documentary that Luke had watched and everything I read about the belief that livers hold the spiritual essence of a body.

Tracie's eyes widen as she realizes what I'm getting at.

"You think the Order cut her liver out because it contained… her spirit?" she asks.

I shrug with an excited smile on my face.

"I don't know. Maybe. I mean, it's worth checking out."

"So, this is a common thing to do?"

"I wouldn't say common but it happens."

Luckily, I had done a lot of research last night. Probably too much since I only got a few hours of sleep.

"Actually, a lot of cults and weird religious sects use livers in their rituals," I say. "People think the heart is where the soul is, but there are a number of groups that believe it's in the liver. I think that way of thinking originated in Mesopotamian civilizations.

From what I've read, people from various civilizations have worshipped the body and its various parts in ways that I can't understand. Maybe it's because I've seen so many bodies in so many different states. Cold and still. Ripped open and bloody. Precisely cut open and pale on a medical examiner's table.

I don't assign any meaning to organs besides their scientific processes, but it's not like I'm the most spiritual person in the world.

My view is clear-cut, so I guess I'll never fully understand how someone can slice another person's liver out of their body for a spiritual reason.

"It's hard to believe these types of rituals still happen today," Tracie says as she shakes her head in disbelief. "The Order is just some wellness cult. Sure, they do weird things, but I don't know if they're capable of something like this."

"We can't underestimate them."

As a detective, I have to let go of my judgments early on, even if that's hard to do. I am human after all. I wanted Connor to be responsible for this and I felt like he had enough motive to kill his ex-girlfriend, who supposedly didn't want anything to do with him. However, I can't think of any reason why a boy from Iowa slinging drugs would want his ex-girlfriend's liver.

He already seems wary enough about selling opioids. I doubt he has the stomach to sell a liver. This is the work of someone with a twisted mind and a hard stomach.

"What are we going to do when we get there? Ask them where they keep the livers?" Tracie scoffs.

A smirk crosses my face.

"I doubt they still have it. Maybe they burned it. Or ate it," I say and a horrified look fills her face. "I just want to look around and see if we find anything interesting. Ask a few questions. Get a read on them. That sort of thing."

Tracie releases a slow breath as she nods.

"Fine. I guess we don't know much. I mean, we read all of the documentation and talked to some people, but Elijah still seems like a mystery."

That's why I'm suspicious of him. People treat him like some sort of god, but he's just a man. I need to see past his calm, collected façade and figure out who he is underneath all of that. Is he just a leader or is he a murderer as well?

"Because he is. He's acted supportive of us and remorseful over Emilia, but I don't know how this guy operates. Maybe he has abusive tendencies. A master gaslighter," I suggest.

"You'd think they'd do something with the whole body. Like burn it on a pyre," Tracie says. "That seems more in line with practices that I've seen in movies."

I haven't dealt with many cults in my time as a detective. All I know is that that man wields a lot of power and influence.

Tracie scoffs before her shoulders slump slightly.

"Whoever it is, I feel like we've stared the murderer in the face," Tracie murmurs as she peers out of the windshield. "That gets me every time."

And that's the hardest part of the job. Feeling something in my gut and not being able to prove it. It's a constant battle, a race to get the evidence you need.

The freeway in Southern California is a beast all its own. Cars race by, weaving in and out of traffic, their horns blaring impatiently. Billboards tower over the road advertising everything from fast food to amusement parks. The sun beats down on the asphalt, causing the air to shimmer and dance with heat waves.

As I speed down the freeway, the world around me blurs as I focus on the road ahead, my hands tight on the steering wheel. The car hums with power, its engine a steady roar beneath me.

The traffic begins to thin out again. When the road twists and turns, the scenery becomes a blur of green and brown.

Despite the beauty of my surroundings, my mind is elsewhere. I'm consumed with the case, my thoughts racing as I try to piece together the evidence. My gut tells me that something is off, that the pieces aren't fitting together the way they should.

As the miles tick by, my frustration grows. It's hard enough to solve a case when you have all the evidence, but when you're missing a crucial piece, it’s nearly impossible, but I won't give up. I know that the answers are out there, waiting for me to find them.

That's why I'm speeding down the highway, the sun glinting off the hood of my car. I'm on a mission, driven by a need to solve this case and bring the killer to justice. The two-hour drive stretches out, feeling like an eternity given where I'm going and what I'm trying to do.

"We're going to put him behind bars," I say in a determined voice.

"Who?"

"Whoever did this."

A small laugh breaks from Tracie as she shakes her head.

"I'm glad to have you as a partner, Carr. The others at the station… they don't have your sense of humor or your proactiveness."

My eyebrows lift slightly in surprise. I didn't expect a compliment, but it does mean a lot to me. There are some police officers that are not as driven. They're the ones that let cases go cold when they shouldn't, and the ones I don't want to work with. I've pitched a fit before over bad partners, which has coaxed the captain to not bother with giving me someone that I'll outpace.

Admittedly, he did a good job this time linking me up with Tracie. She matches my energy, and even if she challenges me or questions me, she gets my mind working. Constant speculation helps in complicated cases like these.

"You too," I say, unsure of how to properly put my feelings into words. She's a good partner. Hopefully, she can sense that from me. I'm sure she's heard that I'm not the easiest person in the department to work with, but she agreed to see it through regardless.

That already tells me enough about her character.

Tracie merely smiles and turns back forward, her gaze lingering on the passenger side window as we pass by other cars and exit signs.

I check the time on my car's dashboard, seeing that we have about an hour and a half left to go. Drawing in a deep breath, I prepare myself for the rest of the drive, hoping that all of this time and effort isn't going to go to waste. Tracie and I have been putting our all into this case, losing sleep, and our minds a little.

If we can just push a little more, we may make it to the end yet.

32

Emilia

Three Weeks Before Death

"And exhale. Wonderful!"

A shaky exhale broke from me as I lowered my arms from above my head, a burning sensation coursing through my body. Sweat glistened on my forehead as I relaxed, thankful that my hot yoga class was finally over. It made me feel good afterward, but it certainly pushed me to my limits. I couldn't remember ever working out so much in my life until I joined the Order, but I knew that this was good for me.

Everything they encouraged me to do was good for me, even if it was difficult.

"Thanks, Lottie!" Madison chirped as she waved goodbye to our instructor.

I placed my hands on my hips above my white leggings, taking in the sunlight. Madison and I stood near the pool of Elijah's mansion. I loved escaping to Santa Barbara for a little while, soaking up the sun and taking care of my body.

I truly started understanding how terribly I was treating my body when I joined the Order and learned so many new teachings. Even little decisions like staying up too late or eating an extra cookie could have negative impacts that I would have to suffer later on.

If I took care of myself now, my future self would thank me.

Pain now. Gain later.

"I'm done," I breathed out as I turned to Madison, who still looked good even with sweat glistening on her face.

Madison laughed as she tightened her ponytail, her black tank top and tight athletic shorts hugging her slender figure. We both had lost a good amount of weight during the last month, shedding off unnecessary pounds and reducing the amount of inflammation tainting our bodies.

I hadn't been this skinny since I was a lanky teenager. It was nice fitting into an extra small again, and a lot of people had already given me plenty of compliments. Obviously, the program was working.

"All of this is negative, sick energy leaving your body," Madison said as she gestured to the sweat coursing down our faces. "It's important to get it out."

"Even if it makes my legs want to give out," I replied with a light laugh.

Madison bumped her hip against mine.

"Come on. Let's go inside. I'll make us a green juice. It purifies our bodies of toxins."

When I first moved to LA, I tried a green juice or smoothie or whatever from a health food place, but I hated how it tasted. It was like someone threw grass and water into a blender and then served it to me. However, Madison managed to work some sort of magic when she made hers, and it actually tasted pretty good.

"Sounds good. I just need something cold," I replied before following her inside.

Madison led me through the multi-story maze that was Elijah's house, taking me around the corner and through the dining room to the large, modern kitchen with as many appliances as you could dream of. She opened the stainless steel, touch-screen fridge and pulled out a few items to set on the marble counter.

I took a seat at the island and redid my messy bun, raking my fingers up the back of my neck to collect any loose hairs. My eyes swept around the kitchen as I took in everything. I couldn't believe I was in a place like this, going on a journey that I never expected.

Hollywood was full of bad influences, and I had partaken in some things that I shouldn't have. It was so easy to get mixed up with the wrong crowd and participate in risky behaviors. I had been teetering on the edge of getting wrapped up in that culture when I was approached by the Order. According to them, my soul could still be saved and enlightened if I were willing to change. To give myself over to their rules and teachings.

I was suspicious and wary of Elijah and the others at first because I'd heard horror stories about weird religious sects, but I gave them a chance to show me what they were about. They explained the levels to enlightenment to me and showed me how much happier and healthier they were since they'd joined. With the stress from my growing fame and trying to find my place in Hollywood, I was in a vulnerable spot that they were able to sense.

So, I joined and didn't regret my decision. I exercised, ate better, meditated, and connected with others who were on the same spiritual journey. That kept me grounded, and it was nice making a close friend like Madison.

"I got invited to another one of Landon's parties," I said as Madison cut up some celery.

Madison wrinkled her nose in dismay.

"You need to cut contact with him. He's a scummy producer who just wants to sleep with you," she muttered.

I knew she was right. I mostly talked to Landon because he was a good entertainment industry connection, but he was starting to be too much trouble for me to handle. When we were together, he always came up with some sort of excuse to touch me or whisper something in my ear. It had started making me feel uncomfortable, and I had a feeling being around him where there were drugs and alcohol wasn't a good idea.

I didn't want to be a party girl anymore.

When I first moved out to California, I went to every party I was invited to so that I could make valuable connections. Unfortunately, my focus started to slip from business to having fun with people I didn't even really know. Alcohol made me make questionable decisions.

"Yeah, you're right. I'm done with that part of my life," I said with a sigh. I had been doing a lot of trimming, cutting out the excess and the bad. Landon was part of that.

Madison looked up at me with a smile on her face.

"You know, I'm really proud of us. We're so much better than how we were before," she said. "No more drinking or drugs. No more crazy parties. Just health and wellness."

I smiled back and nodded. So many people asked me what kind of diet I was on or what my workout routine was, but I couldn't spill any of the program's secrets. We were a tight-knit group, and Elijah told us to keep things that way since we were a chosen few. I didn't want to step on any toes and get kicked out, so I kept my answers vague.

At least I could talk about it with Madison.

"And we're only going to get better," I pointed out. Madison had been on this journey longer than me, but I could see us doing this for years.

Madison dumped the cuts of celery into

Elijah's Vitamix before letting her shoulders slump.

"If only everyone could do as well as us. I wish Nicole was still here."

I frowned as I thought about her disappearance from the Order. It was so sudden, confusing all of us. Following the program and all of its rules was difficult and some people did quit, but they didn't just… vanish. According to Elijah, Nicole went home, but I wasn't sure if that was actually true.

"Me too. She was really nice," I murmured as I peered down at the island, tracing a few swirls in the marble with my forefinger. "Do you think anything specific made her leave?"

Madison shrugged as she washed kale in the sink to my right.

"I'm not sure. I just think she wasn't strong enough to continue on the path. Pursuing all the steps toward enlightenment isn't for the weak. That's why Elijah is so particular about who he allows into our group. He really thought she'd make it. We all did."

I did notice that Nicole's participation was a bit half-hearted before she left. It was like she was gradually worn down, but I didn't know what drew her away from the path she was supposed to be on. I thought she knew that she wasn't alone and that there were people who could help her.

I had moments of doubt as well and ran into my own personal obstacles, but Elijah, Madison, and the others were always willing to help me work through them. It was a shame that Nicole didn't reach out when she began struggling.

"I hope she's okay," I said.

After drying the kale, Madison walked over to me and took my hands, giving me a small smile.

"I know you worry about her, but don't lose sight of yourself and your goals. It's best that we separate ourselves from her. She might bring damaging energy into our lives."

Guilt radiated through me as I looked away from her.

"I… I might've tried to call her the other day," I said, watching Madison's eyes grow bigger. "I just wanted to make sure that she was okay, but she never got back to me."

Madison held my gaze for a few seconds with a hardened expression.

"Emilia, you can't do that. You can't talk to ex-members."

I nodded in understanding, my face flushing

slightly from embarrassment. I knew that I shouldn't have done that, but Nicole had been nothing but kind to me. I just wanted to make sure that she was home safe and that nothing bad had happened.

"I won't do it again," I promised.

Madison eyed me for another few seconds before letting go of my hands and returning to the cutting board on the other side of the island.

"Good," she said. "It's not safe for us."

I quietly nodded and watched her prepare the rest of our green juice, tossing in ingredient after ingredient. Before she pressed the start button on the blender, she turned to me.

"Can you grab my phone real quick? It's in the living room," she asked with a smile.

At least she wasn't upset anymore. At times, it felt like I was walking on eggshells around Elijah and the others of the Order. I didn't want to mess up and be booted out when I had been working so hard to become more involved.

"Of course," I said before getting off the stool and heading to the living room.

Usually, other members hung out here or outside, but the mansion was quiet today. I looked at the glass coffee table and the tan loveseat, spotting Madison's phone on the armrest of the leather couch. I grabbed it and went back to the kitchen, hearing quiet voices talking.

When I stepped through the door to the kitchen, I spotted Elijah standing next to Madison as she put the lid on the blender's pitcher. My heart jolted in surprise at the sight of him. It was his house, but I didn't see him much.

"Oh, hello," I greeted him. His eyes were so intense it felt like he could see right through me. Did Madison tell him I had called Nicole?

Elijah smiled and moved toward me, moving so gracefully he was almost floating. When he reached me, he cupped my face gently in both of his hands and gazed into my eyes.

"I'm glad to see you here, Emilia. I'm so proud of the progress you've been making lately."

I almost forgot how to breathe. He wasn't upset. He was actually proud of me. Everyone strived for Elijah's approval because he was deeply respected. He did so much for us and was always there to listen to our needs and concerns. We all did our best to make him happy and to show him that his efforts were appreciated.

"Thank you so much. I've been working really hard," I said catching my breath. "But I can work even harder. I'll do whatever it takes."

I had been doing so many workout classes, cleanses, and meditation techniques to try to get myself closer and closer to enlightenment. I had been feeling so good lately that it seemed like I was finally getting close.

Elijah patted my cheek softly and affectionately before turning to look at Madison with a grin on his face.

"She's almost ready," he said before walking out of the kitchen.

I shot Madison an excited look as I hurried over to her, my heart racing.

"Am I close to the end of the path?" I asked in a hushed voice, not wanting him to know that I was freaking out.

Elijah always spoke about the peace and happiness that was found at the end of the path to enlightenment. How all of our stress and bad energy would be cleansed from our bodies and souls.

It was the way we were meant to live, but there was so much bad in life. So many distractions. It was easy to lose ourselves.

Madison leaned her head against mine with a proud look on her face.

"Seems like it," she said before pressing a button.

The vortex of the blender was hypnotic, spinning the green flesh around and around, the blades slicing through everything with ease. A loud whirring noise filled the kitchen as we leaned against each other and watched. The powerful blades suited with serrated edges spun and chopped up everything in their path. They tore through the skins of the fruits and vegetables and peeled them away from the seeds. A little violence in order to achieve something good.

As the blender continued, I couldn't help but feel a sense of foreboding. It was as if the whirring noise was a premonition of what was to come. I tried to shake off the feeling, chalking it up to my overactive imagination.

I had to take the bad with the good, but all that mattered was what came in the end.

I couldn't wait to see what was in store for me.

33

Kaitlyn

When we arrive at Elijah's mansion, I don't pull into the long driveway that slopes upward. The embodiment of the California dream, it boasts a blend of Spanish revival style architecture and contemporary elements.

I stop on the side of the road and turn to Tracie, who sucks in a deep breath.

"We have to find something," I say. I'm certain that this house contains the answers that we are seeking but first we'll have to deal with Elijah and those he controls. They're our sources of information, but they may be distractions as well.

Tracie and I will have to work together to do a subtle deep dive to uncover anything that's hidden from plain sight. We need to find anything that Elijah is trying to hide.

"We will. If this group is truly behind Emilia's murder, that's a lot of secrets to hold in. One or two are bound to spill out, and we'll expose the rest."

We are being optimistic but I'm not so sure it's going to be that easy.

The bright sun beats down on my windshield, warmth laying across my skin like a blanket. I tug at the collar of my black blazer, sweat threatening to break out on my forehead. Maybe it's not just the sun that has me drenched.

"Let's do it," I say before getting out of the car.

We approach the entryway, which features subtle geometric patterns that add visual interest without overwhelming the design. A discreet handle integrated into the door itself offers a seamless and minimalistic touch.

The entrance is framed by large floor-to-ceiling windows on either side, allowing ample natural light to flood the entryway and provide breathtaking views of the Santa Barbara coastline. These expansive windows have sleek black aluminum frames giving an unobstructed vista.

I press the bell and wait. Each second that passes, my heartbeat grows louder and louder as it echoes in my head. It takes a minute before I can make out a blurry shape walking through the foyer.

The door swings open, and Madison pops up in the doorway. The moment she sees us, her eyes grow a degree bigger out of surprise.

"Oh! Hello, officers. What a pleasant surprise."

I wasn't exactly expecting to see her. Does she live here? If not, how often does she visit?

"Is Elijah here?" I ask.

Madison parts her lips to answer, but footsteps sound behind her.

I lean to the side and catch sight of Elijah Nova as he strides toward us, wearing a linen tunic and loose, white pants. Every time I've seen him, he has always been calm and collected. In control. Today is no different.

"Elijah," I greet him with a small nod and a straight face.

"Good to see you again. To what do I owe the pleasure of this visit?" Elijah asks looking at both of us.

Madison steps back to let him take the lead,

joining her hands together and focusing her eyes on him. It's like she's entranced.

"We just have a few more questions for you if you don't mind," Tracie replies with a polite smile. "May we?"

Elijah stares at us for a second before taking a step back and holding his arm out to motion for us to come inside.

"Of course. Welcome," he says.

The foyer is adorned with a landscaping feature. There's a minimalist water fountain burbling softly, which adds a touch of tranquility to the space.

I head inside, following Madison as she leads us deeper into the house. In the den, five young women are hanging out, seemingly relaxed and at ease. The room is stylishly furnished with sleek, minimalist furniture, adorned with sharp lines and monochromatic tones. On the surface, the scene looks innocuous enough.

But my stomach feels uneasy.

On the low coffee table in front of them, glasses filled with vibrant green juice glimmer in the soft lighting. The liquid appears refreshing, but a sense of unease lingers in the room.

"Are you here about Emilia or Nicole? Both

of them passing has been very difficult on all of us," Elijah asks walking ahead.

"Emilia," I reply.

Elijah nods and looks back once, focusing his gaze on me. The heavy tension between us is undeniable.

"I think about her every day. She came by here a lot, and despite her simply being a guest, this place feels emptier than before because her presence will never grace it again," he murmurs with a sad shake of his head. "I hope you find the person who murdered her in such a cruel manner."

"Don't worry. We're working on it," I say as our eyes lock.

The grieving, vulnerable mask he's putting on isn't fooling me. The hard part is wading through all the falseness to find the truth.

"Good," Elijah replies, seeming to put more force into the word.

Silence follows as tension sizzles in the still air. I need to get him talking, but he's a hard man to read. Finding the right approach isn't easy, especially with multiple sets of eyes boring into me.

"Your house is lovely," Tracie states,

changing the mood of the conversation. We are here for answers and, in order to get them, we need Elijah to open up.

"We are very lucky to have it."

"Is it yours?"

"Oh no, it belongs to the Order."

"I didn't realize the Order was so successful," she adds, trying to be tactful. What's not lost on us is that this is a multimillion-dollar house belonging to a seemingly nonprofit religious organization which undoubtedly does not pay a penny in taxes.

Elijah chuckles faintly.

"Well, we are very fortunate. We have a lot of people who believe in our cause. Would you like a tour?"

An official tour is not going to uncover anything, but it might offer up some clues.

"That sounds great," I reply. "I've heard a good way of getting to know someone is by seeing their home. All the little details are telling."

"I try to incorporate my values into my space. Peaceful. Welcoming. Safe," he says gesturing and smiling at two women sitting at the dining table.

The women smile back. When one of them

pushes her hair away from her face, her collarbones jut out. They're both so thin, their tank tops and shorts barely fit. Despite their beauty, their dry hair frames their thin faces, and their eyes seem… glassy.

It takes everything in me not to pitch a concerned look to Tracie, who I'm sure is noticing these worrisome details as well. It's not rare to see incredibly thin women in Southern California. However, something is different about the women here.

"Would you two like a glass? I just juiced some celery, cucumbers, and green apples," Madison asks as she motions to the kitchen island behind her. That's when I see the expensive blender and a cutting board littered with excess celery hearts, cucumber ends, and apple cores.

I love a good smoothie and my mouth is parched.

"Sure. Thank you," I say, as my mouth waters for a taste.

Madison perks up and opens the sleek cabinet. She fixes two glasses and hands them to us.

"Enjoy! We drink this stuff all the time! It's so good and cleansing."

I plaster a smile on my face and nod before turning to Elijah.

“Lead the way,” I say, wanting to get this tour started.

Elijah takes us out of the dining room and up a flight of stairs to the second floor.

“I recently added a meditation room for everyone to utilize. There are blackout curtains and a speaker for music and podcasts,” he explains as he opens a door to show us a dark room with foam flooring.

“So, you allow your members to have free rein of your house?” Tracie asks.

Elijah nods.

“Sharing is an emphasis in our program. We’re all on the same journey to enlightenment, so we help each other in any way that we can."

After he shows us a few more rooms, which don’t spark my interest, I grab the opportunity to branch off on my own.

“Can I use your bathroom?”

Elijah pauses and gestures ahead.

“Take a right, and it’s down that hallway.”

I give him a grateful nod.

Before I turn right, I pause and glance behind me, watching Elijah take Tracie into another room. I hook a left and go down another hallway, seeing closed doors on each side.

I quietly walk past a few rooms, pausing to listen at each door to see if I can hear anything. I'm not expecting much but I have to give it a try.

When I make it to the third door, I lean close only for the door to swing open, making me jump back in surprise as a young woman stares at me in shock. We're both spooked by each other for a second, my hand immediately resting on my holster out of instinct.

The woman's eyes remain wide as she glares at me, seeming frozen in place. She is in her early twenties, and she's even thinner and frailer than the other women downstairs. Her green eyes shift to the juice in my free hand, and she swallows hard.

"You shouldn't be drinking that," she whispers.

My blood runs cold at the sound of her hushed voice.

"Why?" I ask in a matching volume.

The woman looks down at my gun, a shaky breath leaving her dry, cracked lips as a few strands of red hair fall against her forehead.

"They're drugging people," she says as her

eyes start to glisten with tears. She looks up at me pleading. "Please help me. Get me out of here."

I can hardly hear her hushed pleas over the sound of my thudding heartbeat. I set down the green juice and reach out to her, putting my hand on her back and ushering her down the hallway.

I have so many questions but there's no time for any of them.

"Stay close. I'll get you out," I say.

I peek around the corner to see that Elijah isn't in the hallway. I can' hear him in the other room, so I keep my arm around her and rush her down the hallway. Just from having my palm on her back, I can feel the indentations of her spine, my stomach flipping. Who knows how long she's been living like this.

We carefully make our way down the stairs and reach the foyer, our footsteps lightly echoing against the hardwood floors as we make our way toward the front door. I hate to leave Tracie by herself, but she can hold her own until I can get this girl somewhere safe.

We only make it halfway before a slim, dark-haired woman who would be beautiful without that sneer, emerges from another room. It's connected to the foyer and stands in between us and the front door. Her smile is so stiff her lips look like they're made of plastic. She fixes the woman next to me with a hard, pointed stare.

"Amber, you shouldn't be out of your room."

34

Kaitlyn

Things have taken a turn. But I stand firm, steadfast in my determination to protect Amber. With unwavering resolve, I position myself as a shield, guiding her behind me, and fix a penetrating gaze upon the woman in question.

"She can be wherever she wants," I say. "You need to step out of the way and let us pass. She wants to leave."

A soft, derisive laughter escapes the woman's lips, accompanied by a dismissive shake of her head. Her demeanor suggests an air of superiority, as if she holds some secret knowledge.

"She can't. She made a commitment," she replies before looking back at Amber. "Right? You wanted to be here. You wanted to find enlightenment."

Amber grabs the back of my blazer in tight handfuls, her forehead pressing against the back of my shoulder as if she's trying to hide. I reach back, placing a reassuring hand over hers, silently urging her to hold on. Amber's forehead presses against my shoulder. My resolve to protect her deepens.

"It doesn't matter what she said before. She wants out now. You need to get out of the way!" I snap as I push back the bottom of my blazer to show my gun holster. I didn't come here to play around, and I don't care about being polite any longer. She'll either move out of the way, or I'll run right over her.

The woman puts her hands up to try to calm me down.

"You don't understand. You're… impure," she says. "You are tainted with bad energy."

I can only stare at her in confusion and bewilderment as she rattles off words that I doubt she truly understands.

"Because of people like you and Elijah," I grit out, anger flushing through the whole of my body. "Because you don't care about anyone but yourself."

"What's going on?"

I look over my shoulder to see Elijah and

Tracie hurrying down the stairs with Madison. I grab Amber's hand, coaxing her to turn to the side and take a few steps back.

"She needs help. She's leaving with us," I say to Tracie.

Tracie steps away from Elijah and moves to my side, providing Amber with extra cover and protection. She holds a hand out as Elijah and Madison step closer.

"You need to stand back!" she shouts.

Elijah puts his hands up innocently as Madison stays close to his side, her eyes flashing from us to him rapidly like she doesn't know what to do.

"Everyone, let's just calm down," he says in a slow, steady voice.

"Why is she not allowed outside of her room?" I ask narrowing my eyes.

Elijah focuses on Amber, who is cowering between Tracie and me.

"She has free access to the entire house. But in times of high stress, it's recommended that they rest in their rooms. She's been worried and overwhelmed lately given the demanding nature of the program."

Elijah knows all the right things to say. He has an answer for everything.

But the joke is on me. I don't have any evidence of any crime whatsoever and that's pissing me off.

"What are you forcing her to do? All of these women are borderline malnourished!" Tracie says.

"A healthy, cleansing diet and exercise is part of the program, along with group meetings and meditation. Do I ask a lot of them? I do, but great change calls for great sacrifice."

"Has anyone ever sacrificed their life?" I ask, taking a step closer to him.

He glares at me, inhales swiftly but doesn't respond. This is the first time that I have seen a crack in his facade, if I could even call it that.

More like a hairline fracture.

"She wants to be done. So, she's done," I say in a firm voice. "You can't keep her here against her will."

Elijah gives me a small disingenuous smile.

"Look, we just want to help. Amber has suffered notable hardships in her life. The tragic death of her mother and sister. The loss of her modeling job. She went down a dark path, and I'm helping her follow the light to something greater. She knew what to expect when joining. She even signed a contract."

"No contract allows you to lock her up," I say. "I don't care that you're trying to help. I don't care that you think you're doing the right thing for these girls. You're not their keeper. You will let us walk out of here with Amber, and you'll let anyone else who wants to join her go, too."

"We don't want to go," Madison speaks up. "We're happy here. No one has treated us better than Elijah, and we're all healthier, better people than we were before. Some of us were alcoholics. Drug addicts who sold our bodies."

She sounds programmed. She has heard these words so many times that they've become her mantra. This cult runs off manipulation tactics, and the manipulated transform into manipulators.

And the cycle goes on and on.

"Drinking green juice and meditating won't make you a better person by themselves," Tracie says. "Treating others well is how you become a better person, and you're hurting this poor girl by forcing her to do something she doesn't want to do."

Elijah looks past us at Amber again, giving her a comforting look.

"Amber, we're here for you. We want to help

you and support you. You have no family left out there. No purpose. *We* are your family. Let us show you your purpose."

I almost want to turn around and clamp my hands over Amber's ears so that she doesn't hear this nonsense. All the Order does is seek out vulnerable people and make them dependent on a man who wants to be worshiped like a god. They've broken Amber down even more than she already was, trying to convince her that she's nothing without them.

It's cruel, and it makes me *livid*. Just looking at Elijah's calm face and hearing his slow, droning voice makes me want to tear his hair out, and it doesn't help that Madison and the other woman are gazing at him with stars in their eyes.

I shouldn't have been distracted by Conner. I should've been kicking down Elijah's door and getting Amber and any other trapped woman out of here as soon as possible.

Amber doesn't say anything to him, but I can hear the shakiness of her breathing. She's bordering on an anxiety attack, and I'm afraid in her weak state that she'll pass out if she goes into full-fledged panic mode.

I turn to her and look her in the eyes, placing my hand on her shoulder to steady her.

"Let's go," I say, hoping that Elijah's and Madison's manipulative words haven't gotten to her.

I've worked a number of cases that involve abuse victims, and it never gets easier seeing someone who's an obvious shell of who they used to be. They're constantly in fight or flight mode, and they question their own reactions and decisions because they've been manipulated so much. It's easy for them to get sucked right back into a bad situation, especially if it's all they've known for a long time.

A tear breaks from Amber's left eye and courses along the curve of her cheek as she nods.

"I have to get out of here," she says in a quiet, strained voice.

That's all I need to hear from her. I start to move toward the front door, fully prepared to push the dark-haired woman out of the way if she tries to stop me. However, I pause when Amber actually takes a step toward Elijah, her glittering eyes narrowing a degree.

"I saw what you did to Emilia," she hisses,

disgust dripping from her words. "I'm not going to end up like her."

It feels like time stops. I lock eyes with Tracie, shocked looks filling our faces as we hear the words we've been hoping for all of this time. Confirmation that Elijah is in fact the cause of Emilia Cruz's death, and that there is someone who knows about it. My hand drifts down close to the handle of my handgun, preparing to pull it out of my holster as my gaze shifts back to Elijah.

His demeanor shifts as his shoulders tense and I worry that he's about to bolt.

I open my lips to tell him to get on the ground and then realize that he's not even looking at me. He's looking somewhere behind us, nodding his head to someone I can't see.

A wave of dread washes over me, freezing me in place. I spin around just in time to see two massive men stride into the foyer, their muscular frames encased in sleek black jackets. One sports a bald head, exuding an intimidating presence, while the other's dark hair is slicked back, adding a touch of sinister charm. It's a shock—I had no clue there were other men lurking on this property, besides Elijah.

With every heavy footstep, they draw closer,

their presence suffocating. My heart thumps wildly in my chest as the reality sinks in; they're here to stop me. The gravity of the situation hits me like a ton of bricks, intensifying my desperate need to escape.

Panic sets in as I realize how little time I have.

My mind races, frantically searching for an exit strategy, but their looming figures seem to block every possible route.

35

Kaitlyn

Elijah's thugs seem to move in slow motion, each step hitting the floor with an echoing thud. I don't know whether they are armed or not, but the last thing I want is to start a firefight with innocent bystanders around. Even if Madison and the other woman have fully bought into Elijah's deception, I still can't risk them catching a stray bullet, and protecting Amber is my top priority. Whether or not I am able to get hard evidence that the Order is behind Emilia's death, there is no doubt in my mind anymore.

Elijah and Madison are blocking one way out, the two men approaching are blocking another. The only escape is back the way I came, through the dark-haired woman.

I grab Amber's arm and rush back down the

hall. The dark-haired woman steps in front of me, trying to block me, but the endless dieting and cleansing has left her with almost no muscle mass. I drive my forearm into the center of her chest and knock her against the wall, clearing the space for Amber and me to move.

Behind me, I hear shouting and quick footsteps that sound like Tracie, but I don't look back. I need to get Amber out of danger.

I turn to an open door and push Amber through. Two gunshots ring out behind us, one bullet splintering the frame of the door just above my head as I dive into the room. Rolling and leaping back to my feet, I see Tracie headed in another direction, running flat out.

I quickly glance around the room, some odd part of my brain noting that it appears to be a study, comfy chairs, bookcases, low tables. Then I see that there is another door leading out.

"Come on!" I say, feeling Amber resist, her muscles have deteriorated so much that even that brief sprint down the hall has fatigued her. I know she's weak, but we're literally running for our lives.

"I'm trying," Amber replies, sounding on the verge of sobbing as she picks up her pace. Her breaths puff in and out weakly.

I hear one set of heavy, thumping footsteps behind me as one of the guards trails me. The other must've followed Tracie, worry sparking in the back of my mind. She's a capable officer, but she's also my friend. And a big man with a gun is trying to chase her down.

In times of danger, it can be hard to dodge fear, but luckily, there's something magical called adrenaline that tells me exactly what to do to stay alive. Every human has survival instincts. Those who listen to them have a better chance at making it out alive, and I'm not dying today.

I launch us through the door and down a hallway, dragging Amber into one of the guest bedrooms and shutting the door behind us. I twist the lock, but I doubt this flimsy thing is going to keep them out for long. Still, it will buy us time.

"Lay down here," I whisper as we crouch behind the bed that's to the right of the door.

Amber lays on her stomach, visibly shaking as she turns her head to look up at me.

"You're here because of Emilia, right?" she asks.

I peer down at her as I take my gun out of its holster, clicking off the safety.

"Yes. What do you know about what happened to her?"

Amber closes her eyes for a second like she's trying not to sob or throw up. Or both.

"I only realized something was going on when I caught Madison putting stuff in Nicole's green juice," she whispers. "I thought it was dandelion oil or something, but it wasn't."

I now realize why she told me not to drink it. There's no telling what Madison had put inside.

"She did the same thing to Emilia?"

Amber nods.

"To all of us. I noticed Emilia started making excuses not to come around as much. Busy filming schedule. Interviews. All of that. When Elijah and Madison weren't looking, she'd just seem… off. Nervous," Amber murmurs as her eyes grow distant. "I should've talked to her sooner."

"She knew," I whisper back.

Amber nods again.

"I went to the hotel to talk to her before the award show because I knew I could catch her there. She told me everything. How they're drugging us to keep us docile. Most of us are too weak to even leave," she says as she looks at her hand, noting how thin and bony her fingers look.

My eyes snap up to the door as I hear the man's footsteps out in the hallway. Doors open and slam shut around us as he checks the rooms, and it's only a matter of time before he realizes that we've locked ourselves in here.

"Emilia told me I needed to get out, but I had to go back and tell my sister," she says before shaking her head. "I never got a chance to reach back out to Emilia because they took my phone. They said I was too distracted to continue my journey."

I take a deep breath and slowly exhale as I register everything that she's telling me. Emilia knew that something was up. She found out that the Order was doing wrongful things, and she must've tried to extricate herself slowly. That seems like the best way to get away from these people.

"Hang tight. I need to call for some back-up," I reply before taking out my phone and dialing 911.

"911, what's your emergency?" An operator answers a few rings later.

"This is Detective Kaitlyn Carr, LAPD. I need officers sent out to 23 Hillcrest Drive. Code 999.

Shots fired. At least two shooters, maybe more. Two officers on the scene." I say, lowering my voice as I hear the man come closer to the door.

"Alright, officers are on their way," the dispatcher says after a few moments. "Are there any civilians in the area?"

"Yes, there's a group of women in the house, but they're not a threat. There's one other man who is dangerous but not armed as far as I know," I reply, falling silent when I hear the knob turn.

Amber whimpers faintly. A heavy thud sounds against the door as someone rams his body against it. Amber covers her mouth with her hand to stifle her cries.

I place the phone in my pocket and crouch low to the ground, positioning my hands on my handgun and preparing myself for the moment he breaks down the door.

Telling from how hard he's ramming himself into it, it won't be too long now.

"Stay down until I tell you to run."

Amber sniffles.

"I'm so stupid for getting myself into this. I hit rock bottom, but somehow dug myself even deeper," she cries quietly.

I frown as a heavy sensation sinks in my chest, hearing the anguish in her voice. She doesn't think she'll make it out of this alive but I'm going to prove her wrong.

"Get ready," I say when the wood starts to crack.

Tears continue to roll down her face, but she positions her hands flat on the floor, preparing herself to jump up and run whenever I tell her to go.

Just when I think the man is about to break through, I hear a commotion downstairs. The man runs off, but the relief that I feel is short-lived. Two gunshots ring out. My heart drops into my stomach.

Those shots either came from Tracie, or they were aimed *at* her.

I know I need to help Tracie but this is my chance to get Amber out. Grabbing her arm, I pull her to her feet.

"You need to go through a window. Once you are out, you head straight to the road. Try to stay out of sight, I don't know if there are other guards on the property."

Amber nods and takes a deep breath as I slide the window sash up.

I lean out and see that the backyard is surrounded by a wooden fence.

"Can you get through that gate?" I ask her as I point at it.

Amber nods.

"I can," she confirms.

I turn to her.

"What's the last thing that you remember about Emilia before she died?" I ask.

Amber frowns and breathes in before speaking.

"I stayed at the hotel during the award show and after party. I wanted a chance to talk to her again, but Elijah and Madison showed up. She had an argument with them out in the hallway, but I couldn't hear what they were saying. All I know for certain is that she was trying to get away from them."

"What did you do after that?" I ask, my words coming out fast. I pitch a look toward the door of the room hoping that the guard stays back.

"I came back. I thought maybe she'd be here, but I couldn't find her. Then I saw Elijah sneak into this secret room in the library. It's behind the bookshelf. I've never been there before."

If I had to bet on anything, I bet that Elijah is hiding down there right now. I open the window and take Amber's hand, helping her onto sill. I marvel that she is able to move with such energy, given that she is nothing more than skin and bone.

"Run around to the front of the property. Officers will be here soon," I say once she's outside.

Amber nods and carefully eases herself down to the grass before taking off as fast as she can to the gate.

I whip around and run toward the closed door of the bedroom, only to stop at the sound of approaching footsteps. My eyes dart around rapidly until I see an alcove near the door. It's my best shot at hiding, so I press my back against the dip in the wall and stay quiet as the door bursts open.

One of the armed men walks into the room, but he doesn't do a sweep of the area because the open window catches his attention. He hurries over and peers out, spotting Amber making a mad dash.

When he puts his knee on the windowsill to try to crawl through, I shout "Hey!" and step out of the alcove.

He jumps back and reaches for his gun.

"Police! Hands on your head."

He makes a move to raise his weapon but I'm faster.

I aim and pull the trigger, sending a bullet right through his arm and another one through the leg. I could have hit him squarely in the chest, but I never want to take a life if I don't have to. Dropping to the floor, he winces in pain.

I kick the gun out of his hand and pick it up, flicking the safety and shoving it in my waistband. Then I hurry out of the room and down the hall, pausing at a corner to listen closely. The sound of ragged breathing seems to come from the living room. I take a chance and run in that direction. My heart leaps into my throat when I find Tracie bleeding on the ground.

Her hand presses against her side, blood starting to seep through from a gunshot wound that's bad but probably not fatal if help gets here in time. She grimaces as she looks up at me, sweat glistening on her forehead.

"I'm okay," she says.

I look past her to see the other guard face down on the rug in front of the couch. Dead. I crouch down next to her and place my hand on her shoulder.

"Help is on the way. Hang in there, okay?" I say.

Tracie nods and points to a doorway behind her.

"Elijah and Madison ran through there," she whispers.

I get to my feet and head that way, peering inside to see that it's the library Amber was talking about. Unfortunately, there are bookshelves lining every wall, but there's one in the back that stands out to me. All of the book covers are the same color. Red.

I move my hand along the covers, figuring if it's anything like the movies, pulling one of the books will open the room. I start lightly tugging on books until one of them resists, prompting me to adjust my grip and pull harder. It doesn't fully come out, only tilting until I hear a click. With more effort, I'm able to pull the shelf forward like a door, displaying a stone staircase that leads downward.

Lightbulbs along the roof illuminate the spiraling staircase, but it's still dim and eerie as I quietly make my way down the steps. As I approach the bottom, I start to hear faint noises.

I raise my gun as I take the last step into a low-ceilinged tunnel with cement flooring and stone walls. The air hangs heavy with a mix of anticipation and dread.

I creep through the tunnel, stepping carefully to minimize the noise of my footfalls. The sound of people talking echoes around the stone walls, but I can't make out he words. It sounds like the voices belong to a man and a woman.

Elijah and Madison.

I am outnumbered, and the two of them may be armed. Clearly these people aren't afraid to use violence. I will have to take them by surprise, create a moment of hesitation that I can exploit.

Around a final bend, the tunnel opens into a circular, cavernous space. The ceiling is domed. Four large candelabra flicker light onto a floor made of misshapen old stones. Elijah and Madison are at the far end of the room, facing away from me. They are chanting together, speaking in a language I don't recognize. In front of them, partially obscured by their bodies, is a weathered, grey stone at about waist height. It is at least eight feet long and has a flat top. My jaw falls open when I see the dark, reddish-brown stains on the pale stone.

Old, dried blood.

The soft glow of candles casts eerie shadows, cloaking the altar in an unsettling dance between light and darkness. The cellar's ambiance feels otherworldly, as if the air itself carries an ominous weight.

In a sinister display, twisted black candles line the flat top of the stone, their wax deformed and melted, dripping down the sides. Their dim glow paints patterns on the walls. Menacing twisted figurines lurk in the corners.

The very oddness of the scene in front of me numbs my mind for a moment. When it finally clicks, I feel a cold knot in my stomach.

It is an altar.

A sacrificial altar.

Next to the altar, stands a cold, stainless-steel table with an array of surgical tools and equipment. The table's surface, polished to a mirror-like sheen, adds an unsettling touch and the metallic gleam of scalpels, forceps and a bone saw makes my stomach turn.

It's as if the instruments and their sharp edges await their next grisly purpose. The tang of antiseptic hangs in the air, mingling with a hint of something more sinister, as if the very essence of fear has been infused into the room.

White noise fills my ears as I drag my eyes to the right to see Elijah and Madison with their backs to me, hastily shoving what looks like money, spiritual items, and other belongings into two duffel bags.

"Police, put your hands up!" I shout as I aim my gun at them.

They whip around and Madison does as I say, her bottom lip quivering slightly. But Elijah looks as calm as ever, reaching over to grab a scalpel instead of following my orders. He places a hand on Madison's cheek and smiles at her before taking a step toward me.

"Put the weapon down!" I say, resting my finger on the trigger.

Elijah's eyes turn to glass with a disassociated haze.

"The time of my ascension has arrived. I shall be reborn in glory," he announces. Before I can respond, he slices the scalpel across his neck, blood pouring down his clothes. His face turns chalk white, and his eyes darken as he drops onto the ground.

Madison begins to scream, her echoes thundering against the walls. Instead of running toward him, she runs towards me, trying to slip past me and up the stairs. I shake off the shock and force myself to move.

I throw my shoulder into Madison, knocking her into the wall. I grab her and force her down onto her stomach, snapping handcuffs on her wrists as she continues to squirm and struggle. Once she is secured, I force her to her feet, down the tunnel and up the stairs, bringing her into the living room just as other police officers rush into the house with their guns drawn.

Tracie looks up at me from the floor, an expression of relief flooding her face. I can tell that her loss of blood hasn't been that significant.

I give her a nod, the corner of my mouth turning up slightly. There's a hell of a mess to clean up, but everything's okay now.

36

Kaitlyn

Two weeks later, I am flat on my back, heat radiating up from the sunbaked sand. As I bask in the Santa Monica sun, I feel a twinge of surprise at how quickly I have been able to put the horrors of that day in Santa Barbara behind me.

I pull myself to a sitting position reluctantly. Luke has already been packing up all our beach gear for a few minutes.

"Alright, I think that's everything," Luke says as he loads the last of our bags into the backseat of his car. He shuts the door and turns to me, a giddy look crossing his face as he grabs my hand and tugs me over to him, cupping my face once I get close enough. "We're getting married tomorrow."

His smile is contagious, coaxing my own out as I place my hands on his sides.

"Yes, we are," I reply, my heart skips a few beats.

I'm actually getting married in a little less than twenty-four hours. Planning the wedding was one of the most stressful things ever, but I get to marry my best friend at last. Anything is worth going through for that.

Luke leans down and presses his lips against mine, our kiss steadily deepening with each passing second. Pulling away, he flashes a smile, resting his forehead.

"I guess we should get going before we get cited for public indecency, huh?" he murmurs.

I smirk and nod.

"We have a lifetime to make up for it," I say before pecking his lips once more and getting into the passenger's seat.

Luke starts his car, pulling away from the parking lot and hitting the road to Malibu. He takes my hand and gives it a squeeze.

"I'm glad you've taken a few days off. You deserve it."

I nod in agreement. I don't make a habit of taking time off work for so long, but Emilia Cruz's case took a lot out of me. It's great to get a win and solve the case, but Tracie and I went through the ringer from day one. After turning in my report and wrapping up the last few details, I knew it would be smart for me to step away, especially since the wedding is this weekend.

Luke brushes his thumb over my knuckles as he glances over at me.

"How's Tracie doing?"

"Good. She is going to make a full recovery and swears that she's strong enough to make it to the ceremony."

I'm just glad her injury wasn't too serious and that she is going to be back in the field soon. Her kids were worried sick, and I made sure they knew that their mom is a badass.

"I look forward to meeting her," Luke quips with a grin on his face. "Any updates from CSI about the cellar?"

I try, unsuccessfully, to suppress a shudder. The image of that blood-stained altar will be burned into my mind forever. The thought of what transpired in that place sends a chill down my spine.

"Some of the blood found on the stone matches Emilia's. The surgical equipment was sterilized, but they found her DNA throughout the cellar and the boat that was registered to the Order, that they used to dispose of her body. There were other victims there as well, but the lab is still trying to match the DNA to missing persons."

This was one of the biggest pieces of evidence in the entire case and places her at the scene of the crime. This was likely where they removed her liver.

"And they still haven't found anything that explained why they did this? A manifesto of some kind, some kind of religious writings?" Luke asks.

I had spent way too much time in that place, immersed in the horrors of the cellar and the grim reality it revealed. It had been a constant battle to reset my mind, to shift my focus from the darkness to the upcoming wedding. But now, as I sit here, taking a moment to collect myself, I can feel a glimmer of hope that I'm finally in a good headspace.

"No. Elijah was certainly… something else. It seems like most of the ideology was just in his head. That probably allowed him to adapt it to whatever worked best at the time. We found a laptop in a nook under the stairs and the search history showed tons of videos about transplants and training videos aimed at hepatologists. The surgeon I've spoken to said that Elijah actually did a pretty good job, considering he never had any medical training whatsoever. Though if you don't care about the victim surviving, I guess it isn't as difficult."

"I still don't understand the why. Why did they remove her liver in particular?" Luke says with disbelief in his voice.

"Do you remember last year; you watched that documentary on 19th century occultism?"

Luke nods.

"Well, something they said resurfaced in my mind when we were processing that cellar. I didn't think of it when I first got the report about the liver from the medical examiner, but that scene…it looked just like something from that show.

Anyway, some of those occultists believed that the liver was the seat of the soul. Ancient peoples used the liver for divination, as well. I think that Elijah had created some kind of amalgamation of occultism and a sort of wellness cult. Scientifically, the liver does a lot of the work of cleansing the body. I mean, they went on and on about toxins and that is sort of what the liver does. I think Elijah may have been pushing these women to go through all this in order to cleanse their livers, and then he harvested them for himsself and his elite, like Madison."

"Such a waste," Luke shakes his head. "What about Nicole?"

"He had kept detailed notes about every woman in the Order and they revealed that according to him, she began to 'stray from her beliefs.' She wanted to go back to her family, but they wanted to keep trying to change her mind. After her death, the notes said that Madison did a good job of following his instructions and her death was ruled as an accidental overdose. She apparently wasn't pure enough to suffer Emilia's fate."

Elijah has done so much damage to so many people, but he couldn't have done all this damage alone. Madison was his primary weapon. She recruited vulnerable women, she drugged them, she manipulated them and she killed them. We have enough evidence and witnesses to put her away for life.

"What about Connor?" Luke asks.

I shrug. A part of me feels bad about how we treated him but he was a suspect and we were looking for the truth.

"He's back in Iowa. I confiscated that notebook and he promised not to come back, but who knows, right?" I shrug.

"You did great work," Luke says. "I know it was hard, and there was a lot of extra pressure on you with the wedding stuff, but you're incredible."

His words make a warm feeling bloom in my chest, heating up my face slightly. He says that kind of thing often and it always means a lot to me.

I see the worst side of people in my line of work, but he shows me the best side that I sometimes forget exists.

A smile crosses my lips as I look at him, memorizing his features and the way that I feel when our eyes meet. It's the little things that get me through each day. There were a lot of bad days while working Emilia's case.

Tracie and I have each earned commendations, and our success has reverberated beyond the precinct. The news outlets have even graced us with their attention. Though I harbor no joy in witnessing Emilia thrust back into the spotlight, subject to the whims of those who obsessively analyze and theorize, I take solace in the fact that a broader audience has become cognizant of the existence of the Order.

Regrettably, Elijah's nefarious organization isn't the only one out there and there are many others, camouflaged within the fabric of society. But I have to remember that Emilia shouldn't just be a cautionary tale. She's also a person, a victim of a tragic situation she never saw coming, and all I can hope is that she can rest and that her mom finds some peace in knowing that her child's murderer will be brought to justice.

However, there isn't enough justice in the world for a dead child. A piece of those who have lost loved ones dies as well; a piece that they'll never get back. One of the hardest parts about finishing up a case is knowing that nothing has changed for the families of the victim or the victims themselves.

Our impact only reaches so far, but I suppose that's better than nothing.

We stop talking about the case and discuss our eventual honeymoon. The thought of going off to an island far away is a dream come true. Unfortunately, we have to delay it a couple of months. I had used too much of my time off in the Pacific Northwest, and even though I have earned some days rest after this case, I still have a lot to make up.

Luke pulls off the road and into the parking lot of the beach club, the tumbling waves and golden sand already in sight. He parks in the front and turns to me.

"Last chance for you to flee."

I respond by cupping the back of his head and drawing him into a tender kiss, feeling his smile press against mine. When I pull away, I shoot him an amused look and shake my head.

"I'm not going anywhere."

It's a big promise, and maybe some people will say that it's an impossible one to keep given the state of the world, but he knows me to my core. I'm not one to give up or take the easy way out. I fight for what I want, and there's nothing that makes me stronger than the love I have for him. Unfortunately, in my line of work, moments of peace are fleeting, and the darkness can never truly be banished; only held at bay for a time.

But this is my wedding.

Nothing bad is going to happen, right?

Thank you for reading the Girl Shadowed. Book 9 will be available soon. In the meantime, **download the FREE BONUS Chapter** and be the first one to find out about my upcoming releases (and get exclusive free content)!

Want to read another addictive mystery thriller with a shocking twist? 1-click Forest of Silence now!

Forensic psychologist and rookie FBI agent Alexis Forrest returns to her hometown of Broken Hill to investigate the disappearance of a missing teenage girl. Returning to this snowy New England town is the last thing Alexis wants to do. She has a strained relationship with her divorced parents whose relationship did not survive the disappearance and murder of Alexis' older sister, or her dad's prison sentence.

The circumstances of this girl's disappearance are surprisingly similar to her sister's yet the local police aren't exactly welcoming to an inexperienced FBI agent sent to help them solve the case. But then another girl, a wealthy student at a prestigious nearby boarding school, is found dead.

Trying to figure out if the two cases are connected and a serial killer is on the loose, Alexis finds herself getting close to all of the people she thought she had left behind forever. One of those people is a high school boyfriend, a long lost love.

The town is full of secrets that want to stay hidden. To make peace with the past, Alexis must unearth them all. What happens when she finds something that puts her in danger? Will

Alexis find who did it or will she become the next victim?

1-click Forest of Silence now!

Want to start reading now? Just click to the next page for an excerpt.

Can't get enough of Kaitlyn Carr? Read the **Girl Hidden (FREE Novella)** now!

Also, check out my other series following Detective Charlotte Pierce! All of the books are currently available on Amazon and FREE through Kindle Unlimited as well.

1-click Nameless Girl (Detective Charlotte Pierce Book 1)

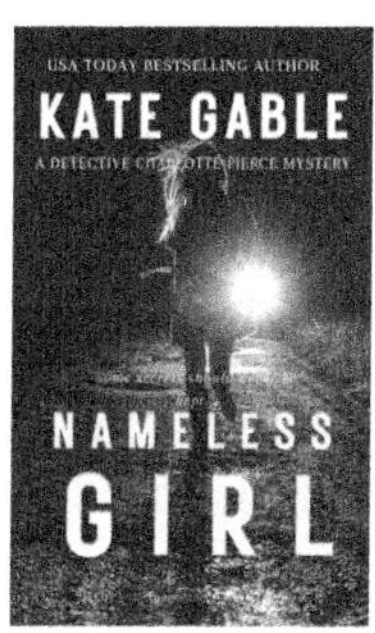

When a 13-year-old girl vanished, her friends have kept certain details of that night a secret. Even though she was only a teenager, this mistake continues to haunt Detective Charlotte Pierce.

Twenty years later, Charlotte attends her

middle school reunion and begins to investigate what happened to her friend that night.

Meanwhile, back home in Mesquite County, CA, another **teenager reports her sister missing and comes home to discover that both of her parents have been brutally murdered**.

Will Charlotte be able to locate the missing girl and find out who killed her parents and why?

Will Charlotte ever find out that truth about what happened to her friend that night?

1-click Nameless Girl (Detective Charlotte Pierce Book 1)

If you enjoyed this book, please don't forget to leave a review on Amazon and Goodreads! Reviews help me find new readers.

If you have any issues with anything in the book or find any typos, please email me at Kate@kategable.com. Thank you so much for reading!

Forest of Silence - Ch 1

This was the last place I wanted to be and the first place they told me to go.

I was always what adults described as an observant girl. Wise beyond my years. Always watching, always aware. The kind of quality that helped earn me a place in the FBI. I saw what others didn't. I was content to let the people around me take the spotlight while I stood behind them, observing.

So it's no big surprise when I return to my hometown for the first time in three years and find it just as divided as ever. As I cross the border into Broken Hill, I'm surrounded by small, sometimes ramshackle homes. In spring and summer, when the trees are full of leaves and the grass is green, it can be pretty out here.

At this time of year, on the other hand? A thin layer of snow coats nearly everything, washing out the color, and the bare limbs that sway gently in the breeze remind me of bony fingers reaching for the sky. A cloudy sky, flat and gray, which only lends to the sense of foreboding. A scrawny dog lopes down the street, lifting its leg and dyeing a patch of snow yellow before moving on. Charming.

It's only a few minutes of driving before the quality of the homes and the cars parked in front of them begins to improve. That's Broken Hill in a nutshell. It starts out sort of grim and sketchy along the outskirts but becomes comfortable and even affluent the further one travels. Here, the streets have been carefully plowed, unlike the slushy mess I rolled through at first. Instead of single story shacks and doublewides, there are modest but quaint single family homes arranged neatly along tree lined streets. I know that they looked dazzling just a month ago when the leaves had burst out in all their colorful glory. The sightseers arrived on schedule, no doubt, jamming up the bed and breakfasts in the heart of town, and generally irritating the locals. The fact that these peepers inject tons of cash into the town's economy doesn't seem to matter as much to the residents as the disturbance of their peace.

Around here, that's what it's all about. Customs. Tradition. Working hard and paddling your own canoe. Typical New England determination at its finest.

I see through it now. The stark difference in class, so obvious when you're coming into town but maybe not as clear when you've spent your life inhabiting it. For most of my early childhood, I grew up blissfully unaware of the poverty on the outskirts of this place. But since my family were squarely middle class, I was also sure never going to attend Hawthorne Academy, the expensive boarding school nestled in the heart of town like a jewel tucked away in a velvet box. Broken Hill High was more my speed.

Still for a little while there, we lived well in the rambling Victorian my parents never did manage to remodel into the bed and breakfast they'd once dreamed of. That was back when they dreamed. Back when they shared a life.

Back before everything fell to pieces.

I check the clock on the dash and snicker. I've been in town for less than ten minutes, and that's where my thoughts headed. How could they not? Everywhere I look, there's a memory that's somehow been ruined by the cloud that's hung over my family for two decades. When I pass the courthouse on Main Street I have to avert my gaze while my stomach tightens and my heart flutters in my chest. It's almost enough to make me pull over and catch my breath, but I have people waiting for me. When I reach a red light I force myself to inhale deeply and let it out slowly. I am not going to let the past get in the way of what needs to be done.

Somebody needs me.

Somebody I can actually help this time.

I hope.

If I looked up the word *idyllic* in the dictionary, it wouldn't surprise me to find a picture of what I now roll through at a reduced speed—this is a busy, bustling part of town, and drivers who don't heed the fifteen mile an hour speed limit end up paying handsomely for being in a hurry. When you rely on tourist dollars the way Broken Hill does, you have to accommodate the public, meaning there's no speeding through the town's commercial district if you don't want to run over a jaywalker. A handful of boutique hotels have popped up in the years since my last visit, while *No Vacancy* signs hang in front of gingerbread Victorians that look almost heartbreakingly beautiful with a touch of snow frosting their roofs and the well-manicured trees and shrubs. It's like something out of a postcard, something Norman Rockwell might have painted.

But just underneath the idyllic surface is a deeper truth. The sort of truth I might never have grasped if it hadn't been for that night. The night we never talk about. The night that managed to leave a footprint on our lives. No matter how we avoid talking about it, it's always there, always in the middle of everything. It changed the landscape of our existence.

I have to force the memories deep down inside once I've reached the police station a few blocks from the courthouse. Like nearly all of the buildings in this part of town, it's a stately, brick structure set behind a wide set of marble steps that freeze over right on schedule every winter. I have to chuckle to myself when I find a man in uniform sprinkling rock salt along their surface. Some things never change.

But I have.

I take a look at myself in the mirror once I've parked in the lot beside the building and I'm almost surprised to find a thirty-year-old woman gazing back at me. Something about being here takes me back to days that should have been simpler and sweeter and might have been if fate hadn't stuck her nose in the middle of everything (if you believe that sort of thing). There's open, frank worry in my hazel eyes and fine brackets at the corners of my full mouth. I'm a little young for wrinkles, but there's no arguing my reflection. I've been dreading this trip from Boston ever since I got word that I was being sent up here. You don't argue with your superiors, especially when you're a rookie agent in your first year with the Bureau.

To my boss, this was a no brainer. I know this town, I know the way people think around here. Sure, I wanted to throw myself on my knees and beg him to send anybody else, literally anyone, but that was only my immediate reaction. By the end of the day, I saw how much sense it makes. And by the following morning, it occurred to me that I might be able to help another family avoid what mine had suffered. I mean, why else did I get into this career in the first place?

I'm quick to run my fingers through my light brown locks before pulling them back into a ponytail. After smoothing down a few fly-aways,

I take a deep, bracing breath and open my door… before recoiling in frozen horror. It can get cold as hell in Boston, but there's something about late autumn in Maine that can steal the air from a person's lungs if they're not prepared. I knew it was going to be colder, but I forgot the particular chill in the air, especially when there's snow on the ground. Even the most innocent breeze can turn frigid, and that's what I'm dealing with as I climb out of the car and navigate the parking lot on foot. There are still icy, slushy patches here and there, but I've managed them with ease before climbing the salty steps and entering the station.

Time to meet the task force.

The desk cop positioned near the entrance lifts an eyebrow when I appear in front of him. I raise my badge, hanging from a lanyard around my neck. "High, there. Agent Alexis Forrest. I'm here to meet with Captain Christopher Felch about the Martin case."

There's no getting around announcing my affiliation. I'm prepared for the disdainful look I get, along with a few muffled snorts from the cops a little further back in the bullpen.

"Well, well." The cop— Officer Fisher, according to the name badge— leans back in his chair and folds his arms. "Aren't we lucky? The Bureau decides to send its prettiest agent to help us do our job."

His words drip in New England drawl; all nasal and full of dropped r's.

Your job? You sit behind a desk and direct people when they come in. Right. Because that would earn me any points. "Can you show me where I can find Captain Felch?"

"Don't fret. He'll find you." And with that, he rotates away from me in his chair, sharing a laugh with his buddies.

So much for cooperation. But that's fine. I'm not here to make friends— and even though I think it might earn me points, I don't see any need to announce that I grew up here.

As it turns out, I don't have to. "Hey, I know who you are."

My head snaps up and I look around before realizing the tall, grinning man is talking to me. He strides my way wearing a big, goofy grin. His golden blond hair gleams in the overhead lights while his blue eyes sparkle. Mr. All-American Boy.

"Me?" I ask.

"Sure."

"And who are you?"

"Andy Cobb, Agent Forrest." He glances around like he's making sure others are paying attention, and there's a sick feeling in my stomach that only gets worse once he continues. "You're the one whose sister was murdered all those years ago, right? And your dad shot the guy on the courthouse steps."

Well, there it is. It was bound to come out eventually, though I didn't figure it would be as loud and obnoxious and generally embarrassing. All at once, everyone's attention shifts to me, and I might as well be ten years old again.

The girl whose sister was murdered.

The girl whose father went to prison for trying to kill the man convicted.

For the next eight years after the terrible night we lost Maddie, I got used to the whispers. The funny looks, the sympathetic frowns. In the twelve years since, I sort of lost the thick skin I built up.

There's no choice but to lift my chin and get through it, because this won't be the last time someone brings up the past and I'd better get used to it. Yet before I can offer a reply, a tall, middle-aged man claps his hands sharply and draws the attention of everyone in the vicinity.

"Let's go. Conference room." His narrowed

gaze sweeps over the room and everyone gathered in it. "It's time for a briefing on the Martin case."

Something tells me I just got my first look at Captain Felch.

Forest of Silence - Ch 2

"Agent Forrest." Captain Felch has a strong grip that he demonstrates when he shakes my hand. "I wish I could say it's a pleasure."

"I understand." As we chat, the room fills with officers who chatter quietly settling in around a long table. Those who can't find a chair line up along the walls. I don't think there's a single one who doesn't give me a look that I would describe as unwelcoming if I were feeling generous. Really, they're flat-out hostile for the most part. I am the living, breathing reminder that somebody somewhere doesn't think they have what it takes to find a missing girl.

Once everyone's gathered, the captain clears his throat. "Everyone, this is Agent Alexis

Forrest. She's our FBI liaison from the Boston office, and she'll be helping us investigate Camille Martin's case."

There's a brief ripple that goes over the room. A few of them— women, all— nod in greeting. Not the men. They would rather sneer and look offended. That's fine. They wouldn't be the first.

Pinned to a corkboard spanning the wall behind us is a blown-up photo which the captain points to. "Camille Martin. Fifteen-year-old sophomore at Broken Hill High. Her parents are both teachers there, and they're convinced she would never have run away. Somewhere between her shift over at *Broken Hill Books and Coffee* and the time she was expected to arrive at the family home, something happened. It's up to us to figure out what."

Beside the photo of the smiling, dark-haired kid, there's a map. "The family's home sits just here." He points to a spot I vaguely recognize as the area I drove through between the trailer park and downtown. Middle class, maybe a little on the poorer side. If both parents earn a high school teacher's salary, I can imagine why. "It's around two miles from the bookshop. Camille was supposed to get a ride, according to the store's owner, but she assured him she could walk. From the way he tells it, her shift ended at five-thirty and the café closed at nine-thirty. It was only the two of them working, meaning he would have had to close the shop to drive her home. The snow fell earlier that day, but it had stopped by then, the wind had died down, and she was sure she could make it easily. As we know now, she never made it home."

He releases a heavy sigh. "That was more than forty-eight hours ago. The only two surveillance cameras set up facing the street happen to be out of order now." A soft groan rises around me. "The rest of the cameras face inside, monitoring customers. All we have is this from the store owner."

He picks up a remote and points it at the laptop set up on the conference table. The image appears on a screen spanning the wall to my left, with a timestamp that reads *5:47 PM.* I recognize Main Street easily, even though the image covers a narrow area. Through the front door emerges the girl in the photo.

Camille.

She's pretty, fresh-faced, smiling when she looks back into the store like she's saying good-bye. She's dressed in a dark polo shirt that I assume was provided by her boss, jeans, and sneakers. She finishes zipping up her puffy jacket and crams a knit hat over her dark tresses, then starts walking with her shoulders hunched like she's trying to adjust to the cold.

Camille. What happened to you?

"We've been through her cell and her laptop. We've combed through her social media. There's still information to be uncovered, but as far as we know from preliminary interviews, she had no plans to meet up with anyone."

I'm like a kid in school, raising my hand slightly to get his attention. "Any family or friends seem withholding or suspicious?"

"They couldn't be more cooperative. Everyone we've spoken to thinks the world of this kid, and they all want to see her come home."

Not to attract even more attention, but I have another question. "You mentioned looking through her phone. Do we have it?"

"We," somebody mutters while someone else snickers.

Captain Felch shoots them a dirty look over the top of my head, and the snickering ends. "We accessed her iCloud account. Her laptop was still at home, but she had her phone on her.

It's missing." Then, like he's anticipating the next natural question, he adds, "Conveniently—or inconveniently, depending on how you look at it— the Find My iPhone feature was turned off."

Of course it was. Now I understand why he looks so tired, almost pained. Girls go missing all the time, and there are no obvious leads so far.

Just like another case I was unfortunately connected to.

My first stop is the most obvious one. Camille was last seen at the bookstore, so that's where I'm headed, walking the couple of blocks rather than taking the car. After sitting in that stifling station with so much judgment bearing down on me, it's a relief to get outside. The air is so cold it burns my lungs, but I welcome the sensation. It centers me.

The first word that comes to mind as I approach the shop is *charming*. Almost annoyingly so. Just like downtown Broken Hill is a postcard of a quintessential New England town, the bookshop is similarly picturesque. There are books arranged in windows outlined in white twinkle lights and decorated with paper snowflakes. A distinct scent of old paper and coffee envelopes me as soon as I open the door.

This isn't the time to take a deep, relaxing breath. I still do for some reason. I've always been a bookworm, and the sight of a small fireplace with a pair of leather chairs arranged in front of it does something to me. All I'd need is a thick blanket and an even thicker book, and I'd be set for the rest of the day. The shelves practically bow under the weight of so many books in every conceivable genre, all of which are listed on cheerful cards taped at the ends of the rows.

“Can I help you find something, ma’am?”

At the sound of that deep voice, I turn away from a row of biographies to find a friendly, smiling face. A smiling face that's much too familiar.

I never did get the owner's name, did I? I was in too much of a hurry to escape the heavy, hostile energy at the station.

Now, I’m staring at my past once again.

“Mitch? Mitch Dutton?” Strange how a name that was once as familiar as my own now threatens to get stuck in my throat.

He looks the same as before. It's almost as if not a day has passed since the last time we set eyes on each other. His light gray turtleneck sets off ice-blue eyes I'd spent hours gazing into in a former life, while his chocolate-brown hair looks as thick and soft as ever. Good thing my hands are in my coat pockets, or else he'd see the way they flex into fists as I fight the urge to reach out and brush a few strands away from his eyes.

His smile. Jesus, it's as heart-stopping as ever. Maybe more so, since he's no longer a teenage boy. He's a man. "Alexis. Holy crap. What brings you here?"

Before I can answer or even suck in a breath, his smile slips away. "Of course. Stupid question."

My attempt at a friendly-if-bewildered grin turns into something closer to a grimace. "You know what I do for a living?"

"What? You think my high school girlfriend left town and I never asked about her?" He lowers his brow, shooting me a knowing look. "Your mom stops in on occasion. She says it's because she's addicted to my cinnamon rolls, but I get the feeling she likes bragging about her daughter."

Lies. She's never bragged about me. Whatever warm, maternal feelings she possessed died with Maddie. But he's trying, and I have to meet him halfway. "She didn't tell me you're working here, but then we don't speak all that often."

"I don't work here. I own the place."

"You do?"

His head bobs up and down, but his jaw tightens like he's in pain. "I should've closed for a few minutes. I shouldn't have let her go."

The agent in me watches this like an outsider, coolly observing his behavior and making note of the pain in his voice.

The ex-girlfriend in me wants to offer comfort. I can't do that. Not yet, at least. I'm here on business. "It's easy to blame ourselves when something awful happens. I'm sure Camille took that walk dozens of times and made it home just fine."

"Thanks." He straightens his posture a little and lifts his heavy brows. "So, what can I do for you, Agent Forrest?"

Captain Felch already announced the store's owner was plainly visible in the store's security footage and that he locked up at nine-thirty, four hours after Camille left the shop. The chances of him being a suspect are slim to none. My relief is palpable. "What can you tell me about

Camille? Did it seem like she was hiding something? Or maybe like she was excited or nervous?"

He shakes his head. "She's a sweet kid, hardworking. She cut out the snowflakes on the window and hung the lights. Usually, a high school kid takes an afterschool job and they show up and do the bare minimum. But she engages with the customers and takes her work seriously. I was planning to offer her full-time hours over winter break and again over the summer."

He speaks about her in the present tense. He has hope. My heart softens while I ask myself why I couldn't have put on a little more makeup today. I wanted to look professional when I met the task force. Nobody told me I'd run into an old boyfriend. I consider letting my hair out but I don't want to look like I'm trying too hard to make an impression.

"We're going to do everything we can," I assure him, though I know damn well the odds aren't in our favor. Two days have passed, and every minute that ticks by makes it less likely we'll find her alive.

"I know you will. Nobody's more tenacious than you."

"You haven't known me in a long time."

His eyes twinkle as he shakes his head. "Not you. You wouldn't change."

Neither has he. He's just as charming as ever. It's almost enough to make me question why we broke up in the first place. But it was a wise decision made by two stupid teenagers. I was going to Boston University and he was staying local and attending the University of Maine. We didn't want things to be complicated.

Mitch checks out a few customers so I hang back and watch out of the corner of my eye while exploring the shop. The front half is devoted to books, while the back is where coffee and pastries are sold. A handful of small tables sit scattered between the café counter and the bookshelves, where people can sit and read while drinking coffee.

"What do you think?" Mitch asks once we're alone.

"I think it's adorable and cozy and the sort of place I'd love to spend an afternoon."

He rocks back on his heels, jamming his ring-free hands into his jeans pockets and grinning, in that familiar bashful way that used to turn my heart to a puddle. "You feel like sharing that review on Yelp?"

For the first time today, I laugh, and he joins me. "I'll get on that. Well, I'd better get moving." There's regret behind my announcement, but I am here for a reason that doesn't involve flirting or reconnecting with an old flame. "I only rolled in this morning, so I haven't yet met the parents."

His expression hardens slightly. "They're really distraught," he says and I can almost taste his sorrow. "Why don't I give you my card in case you have any other questions?"

I have to fight off a knowing grin when he snatches a card from a small display on the counter. "I'll keep this close by," I assure him before tucking it into my coat and trying to ignore how thrilling it was when our hands brushed.

But now is not the time. There's a girl out there somewhere, and I need to focus entirely on that.

Forest of Silence - Ch 3

Some things never change. How many times have I heard that little gem? Coming back home is proof enough of how true that is. There might be new businesses in town, and I drove past two different construction sites on my way to Broken Hill High. Condos, it looks like. Little villages nestled in the heart of a larger village. Time hasn't completely stopped.

But when it comes to the town's public high school, time may as well have stood still. Not only for the past three years since my last visit, but in the twelve years since I graduated. I could easily be parking before class as I pull in, though now I'm in the faculty lot as a visitor. So many memories of what had been came crashing down at once. It's one thing for my presence in town to stir to life so much of what I've tried to squash down and forget. It's another to stare up at the three-story brick building and fight through the sensation of a tidal wave sweeping over me, pulling me down into dark water I haven't dipped a toe in for more than a decade.

But this isn't about me. I remind myself of that as my heavy soled shoes crunch over a film of ice that's formed on top of the snow-covered lawn. This is about Camille. The clock is ticking.

I know the way to the front office by heart, hanging a right after climbing the same fifteen granite steps I climbed every morning on my way into the building. Scent is so evocative. It has the power to immerse us in the past before we know what's happening. The smell of the floor polish is almost enough to knock me back a few steps once I'm inside the front lobby, but I push through, ignoring the curious glances of a pair of giggling students leaving the office before I step inside.

My God, even this is the same, right down to a few of the ladies chatting over their coffee. I clear my throat to get their attention.

"Good morning. I'm Agent Alexis Forrest, and I've been assigned the Camille Martin case.

I was hoping to speak to Mr. and Mrs. Martin, and I understand they're here today." Frankly, I can't imagine why. If my kid went missing a few days ago, the last place I'd want to be is work. Especially if it meant being surrounded by a bunch of kids her age, kids she grew up with.

"Of course, I remember you." I vaguely recognize the woman who speaks, thanks in part to the fact that her hairstyle hasn't changed since I graduated. I don't think it's changed since the late nineties—she uses enough hairspray on her mile-high bangs to keep an entire company in business.

What do you remember? The student, or the girl whose sister was killed? I force my way through a smile instead of asking that ugly question. "Yes, Mrs. Baker, I remember you as well. It's nice to see you. The circumstances could be better."

Her eyes cloud over with sadness that seems to be shared by the rest of the group. Her voice drops closer to a whisper as she explains, "Brian and Tess are probably in the faculty lounge. They have substitutes handling their classes, and they've been camped out in there all morning."

Interesting. "Thank you. I know the way," I tell the ladies, all of whom chortle softly.

The faculty lounge is on the second floor,

meaning I climb a flight of stairs in a narrow stairwell, thankful that there are classes going on. Otherwise, I'd get caught up in the flow of traffic as everyone hurries to their next class. In such a large building— the length of two football fields, if I remember correctly— every second counts. In my junior year, I had to make it from the school's gym at one end of the building all the way to the opposite end for psychology in the auditorium. It's amazing I didn't break my neck sprinting down the hall, getting jostled and bouncing off one backpack after another.

Granted, I would have had a little extra time if I weren't busy making out with Mitch after we got changed out of our gym clothes, but that's another story. That's how kids are. Every second I could spend with him, I was by his side. No question. I can almost taste the mint gum he used to chew nonstop back then. He confessed once that he did it to keep his breath fresh for me.

Not the time, Alexis. This trip isn't supposed to be a fun little walk down memory lane. I'll have all the time in the world to think about Mitch once we find Camille.

The teacher's lounge sits between the girls

and boys bathrooms halfway along the school's west wing. Across the hall is the computer lab. I can hear the typing going on in there, while the sound of faint music floats down the hall from orchestra practice. I wonder how many of the kids under this roof are thinking of Camille now. I wonder if it's hard for them to concentrate.

I knock at the closed door before easing it open. The last thing these people need is somebody barging in on them. They are hard at work, and now I understand why they're here and not at home. They're using the copiers to make posters. Judging by the neat piles already arranged along a table that sits against the far wall, they've been at it all morning.

Mr. Martin notices me first. He's still as good looking as I remembered him, without so much as a hint of gray in his sandy hair. Plenty of girls had crushes on him back in the day. He was the kind of charismatic teacher who engaged his students. He didn't try too hard to be everybody's buddy. His naturally friendly, warm personality shone through. I was always sorry I never had his English class.

His wife, on the other hand, I remember very well. She turns when I clear my throat, and it's like looking at her daughter. Camille inherited her mother's shining dark hair and delicate features, plus the wide, coffee-colored eyes that are now terribly bloodshot and swollen. They both look like they threw on whatever wrinkled clothes they could find this morning. Tess's sweater is inside out. I doubt she'd care if she knew.

"Mr. and Mrs. Martin," I begin softly, offering a sympathetic smile. "I don't know if you remember me. I'm Alexis Forrest, and I now work with the FBI. I've been assigned Camille's case."

"Please. Brian and Tess." Brian extends a hand which I shake firmly before turning to his wife.

Light flares to life behind her eyes. "Of course, I remember you. AP Psychology, right?"

"That's right. I'm surprised you remember me."

"You were one of my favorite students." She barks out an almost silent laugh. "That's the sort of thing teachers tell their old students all the time, but I mean it with you."

"To tell you the truth, I loved your class so much that I ended up studying for my PhD in forensic psychology down at the University of

Virginia. That was my last stop before the FBI. You inspired me."

"That is so nice to hear." She's been smiling for too long. Now it cracks before the light drains from her eyes. "I'm sorry. I'm ... very tired. Do you know anything? Have you heard anything new?"

"Captain Felch gave me a full rundown. I only arrived in town a couple of hours ago." I nod toward a cluster of chairs near a window overlooking the snow-covered football field. "Can we sit down? I promise, I won't take too much of your time."

Brian sits, propping his head on his palms, elbows on his knees. He's the picture of a grieving father. Tess sits beside him and leans against him, letting her cheek touch his shoulder. Now I remember when Camille was born. God, it's surreal, thinking back to when the beloved Mrs. Martin went out on maternity leave. She used to talk about Camille every so often during class, too. And now I'm here to investigate her disappearance.

"I'm only going to ask a few questions, and I'm sorry if they've been asked before. I'm sure you don't like having to repeat yourself."

"It's no problem," Tess whispers. "It might help somehow."

I pull out my phone and open the audio recording app. After making note of the date and time, I launch into my first questions. "What can you tell me about her? What did she do after school? Who was she friends with? Did she have any hobbies?"

"I'll tell you exactly what I told the police; Camille is a good girl." Brian lifts his head, staring at me with eyes so full of pain I want to look away from them. But I can't. I won't. The least I can do is face him and let him know I'm not going to run away. "Straight A's. Conscientious. Plenty of friends."

"And you knew her friends?"

"You know how it is around here," Tess murmurs. "Everyone knows everybody else. These kids, they've grown up in front of us."

"She always hung out with good kids," Brian assures me. "The kind of teenagers you know are going to make something of themselves one day. Like you were."

"Did she ever stay out late?"

They shake their heads in unison. "She was always home by curfew. If she were spending the night somewhere, one of us would talk to the parents to confirm. There was no sneaking around."

On one hand, I'm glad to hear it. On the other, I'm not coming up with many leads based on their descriptions. Surely, Camille can't be this perfect.

What if she is? Too often nowadays, kids end up getting mixed up with the wrong people, usually online. You don't have to break curfew to meet a predator over the internet. "What about her browsing habits? You know kids today and their phones."

"Are you kidding? I tried to take a phone away from one of the kids a few weeks ago and I would swear he was about to have a seizure." But Brian shrugs his shoulders anyway. "She never fought us on turning that thing off when it came time for homework or dinner."

"Believe me," Tess adds. "As teachers, we have to stay on top of the latest trends and threats. What to look for, that sort of thing. If anything, we've been hypervigilant. There were no warning signs."

"She did date a boy last year," Brian murmurs while his wife fishes a tissue from her pocket to wipe her leaking eyes. It's not that she's actively crying— she's able to clearly answer my questions— but the tears roll down her cheeks just the same. "They broke up, but it was very low drama. Camille is not a dramatic girl."

Now we're getting somewhere. "What's his name?"

"Danny Clifton. Decent kid, never any trouble," Brian reports. "Otherwise, we even suggested she date somebody new. With the Soph Hop coming up at the end of the year, we figured it might be nice for her to have a date."

"But she's never very interested," Tess concludes. "Always studying. Pulling shifts at the bookstore to save up money."

"I have one more question, and then I'll leave you to it here. I understand there's a press conference at one o'clock, down at the police station."

Tess nods. "That's right. After that, we want to start papering the town with these signs."

"Did she ever mention anything about anyone following her around? This could be anybody. Customers at the store, kids at school, anyone."

They both wear the same blank look, shrugging. "Never."

"Would you mind giving me the names of

her friends so I can talk to them?" Tess rattles off a handful of names which I make note of before standing and offering them a sympathetic smile. "I'll see you at the station. I'm going to do everything I can."

Now, all I have to do is to find something.

Want to read more? 1-click Forest of Silence now! (Read free through Kindle Unlimited)

About Kate Gable

Kate Gable loves a good mystery that is full of suspense. She grew up devouring psychological thrillers and crime novels as well as movies, tv shows and true crime.

Her favorite stories are the ones that are centered on families with lots of secrets and lies as well as many twists and turns. Her novels have elements of psychological suspense, thriller, mystery and romance.

Kate Gable lives near Palm Springs, CA with her husband, son, a dog and a cat. She has spent more than twenty years in Southern California and finds inspiration from its cities, canyons, deserts, and small mountain towns.

She graduated from University of Southern California with a Bachelor's degree in Mathematics. After pursuing graduate studies in mathematics, she switched gears and got her MA in Creative Writing and English from Western New Mexico University and her PhD in Education from Old Dominion University.

Writing has always been her passion and obsession. Kate is also a USA Today Bestselling author of romantic suspense under another pen name.

Write her here:

Kate@kategable.com

Check out her books here:

www.kategable.com

Sign up for my newsletter:
https://www.subscribepage.com/kategableviplist

Join my Facebook Group:
https://www.facebook.com/groups/833851020557518

Bonus Points: Follow me on BookBub and Goodreads!

https://www.bookbub.com/authors/kate-gable

https://www.goodreads.com/author/show/21534224.Kate_Gable

amazon.com/Kate-Gable/e/B095XFCLL7

facebook.com/KateGableAuthor

bookbub.com/authors/kate-gable

instagram.com/kategablebooks

tiktok.com/@kategablebooks

Also by Kate Gable

Detective Kaitlyn Carr Psychological Mystery series

Girl Missing (Book 1)

Girl Lost (Book 2)

Girl Found (Book 3)

Girl Taken (Book 4)

Girl Forgotten (Book 5)

Girl Deceived (Book 6)

Girl Hunted (Book 7)

Girl Shadowed (Book 8)

Girl Hidden (FREE Novella)

FBI Agent Alexis Forrest Series

Forest of Silence

Forest of Shadows

Forest of Secrets
Forest of Lies
Forest of Obsession
Forest of Regrets

Detective Charlotte Pierce Psychological Mystery series
Last Breath
Nameless Girl
Missing Lives
Girl in the Lake

Lake of Lies (FREE Novella)

Printed in Great Britain
by Amazon

58500382R00199